Minnie Hannah Peck

The View of Roses

Minnie Hannah Peck

The View of Roses

ISBN/EAN: 9783337077907

Printed in Europe, USA, Canada, Australia, Japan

Cover: Foto ©Andreas Hilbeck / pixelio.de

More available books at **www.hansebooks.com**

THE VIEW OF ROSES

BY

MINNIE HANNAH PECK.

—

" I am the rose of Sharon and the lily of the valleys."
—Sol. Song ii : 1.

" Whoso offereth praise glorifieth Me."
—Ps. l : 23.

San Francisco :
PRINTED FOR THE AUTHOR.
1893.

PREFACE.

My main object in publishing this little work is to leave a testimony to what God has manifested to me of his free and precious grace. It is not expected that the masses will even take it up to carelessly lay it aside again. But it is written for the one or two, here and there, who are " poor in spirit," who are "meek and lowly," and who may, in answer to my prayer, find some word of solace, hope or encouragement to urge them onward in their pilgrim journey. A desire to put myself in a true position has given me an autobiographical impulse, and caused me also to mention some facts which otherwise would have been left out.

I have also mentioned the names of many with whom I have been connected or associated. This also arose from a desire to be real with them, and because my heart reached out after them, desiring something as permanent for them as for myself, and that we altogether might add something to the present need of real personages in abiding truths. I now commit this little volume, with all I have and am, to our precious Jesus, praying God to overrule all for His glory.

M. H. P.

CONTENTS.

PART I.

PART II.

viii CONTENTS.

PART I.

EARLY RECOLLECTIONS.

Y FIRST recollections are concerning divine things,—the hallowed associations which cluster around the worship of the living God, whom I learned even in my childhood to reverence and fear. Those scenes which impressed me most were the attendance of meetings for worship by my father and mother and myself with a few country people, who met in a log meeting-house near my father's farm. The distance to be walked was over a mile, through fields and woods, over a swollen stream, crossed on a foot-bridge of some long rails. The ministers who conducted these meetings were the early Methodist pioneers, the name of

Raper being, perhaps, the most prominent. Some United Brethren, also of great zeal, preached at this point. In going to and coming from this little log house, with its board seats and high box pulpit, my steps often grew weary, and my father's strong hand held mine more firmly, and sometimes he took me in his loving arms and made me feel a security and rest which I remember well ; and the sweet old choruses,

"Only let me die happy,"

and

"Canaan, sweet Canaan,
I am bound for the land of Canaan,"

would soothe me to sleep oftimes before we reached our home,—a large two-story frame house in the center of a lovely lawn studded with shrubs and flowers, beside a lovely garden, the fragrant herbs of which I e'en yet breathe in. O, those glory days of sweet, sweet childhood nourished by Christian parents under the.wing of the Heavenly Dove. My mother, O, my precious mother, how hallowed her memory now, though more than fifty years have fled since then, and for sixteen years she has lain under the beautiful green sward of an Ohio cemetery.

Her two first children preceded her in infancy to the better world, and then a brother older than I, my constant companion and protector in play in our tender years. We were the objects of her tender solicitude to train up for God. While young she was wont to tell us sweet stories for our good ; but the one I remember best is the

STORY OF HER SALVATION.

Her father died when she was very young, and her mother, said to be most beautiful, but not a Christian, married a profane man. There were three sisters of them. My mother's name was Priscilla,—a dear old Gospel name. When she neared womanhood the Methodists began holding meetings in their neighborhood at the residence of Mr. Christman, a man of great piety ; and mother and her sisters, Mary and Matilda, attended; and mother and Matilda gave their hearts to God, my mother saying that she took the step for life,—to be a permanent espousal to Christ.

The next morning after she joined the Church her stepfather in a rage came to where she was baking buckwheat cakes for breakfast, by an old-fashioned fireplace, and raising his foot kicked the pan of batter over, and then running to the other sister, who was spinning wool, snatched the distaff from its place and threw it down from the high hill upon which the house stood. The sister, being the unsaved one, told him that if he wanted the distaff he could go and get it ; she would not ; and then my mother, having adjusted the pan of batter, went with joyful heart to the bottom of the hill and procured the distaff and brought it to its place. So much for Christian grace.

This ended the scene of anger for that time. He tried in every way to get Priscilla, his favorite stepdaughter, to give up the meetings and dear old father Raper's preaching, and at one time came to her after one of the grand old meetings had just ended and threw a cup of water in her face, saying, "I baptize you," etc., using a profane sentence. None of these things moved the saved young girl. She knew Him whom she believed. As mother grew to womanhood her stepfather longed to mate her with one of his own sons,—Mordecai Crockett,—but mother had seen and loved at first sight a young man, a neighbor, by the name of Daniel Oakes, and to him she soon pledged her loving heart.

Now these were trying times, for he was not a Christian, yet she determined he soon should be ; and her prayers were speedily answered, and they wended their way heavenward together, and were married, though not at home, as that was refused them, and a sister then married made them a merry wedding ; and from there they went to my mother's farm, given by her grandfather Freeman, where soon my father erected a commodious house, which was at once opened for the reception of ministers of the Gospel of Jesus Christ. A hallowed home it was to little Samuel and Hannah, with their love of the meetings, and the preacher's visits, with the singing and praying and kind words and pleasant stories, where thrift and neatness and plenty prevailed, with all hands joining in honest toil.

SACRED POEM.

"Salvation, O, thou joyful sound,
    What pleasure to our ears,—
A sovereign balm for every wound,
    A cordial for our fears.

Salvation, let the echo fly,
    The spacious earth around ;
While all the armies of the sky
    Conspire to raise the sound.

Salvation, O, Thou bleeding Lamb,
    To Thee the praise belongs ;
Salvation shall inspire our hearts,
    And dwell upon our tongues."

EARLY TRAINING.

My brother and I were sent to the common school near home until we quite finished the common branches of study. How merrily our school days passed under sunny skies or over snowy paths as we wended our way with books and dinner-pail. Early and late, year in and year out, the lessons were learned and said ; and then our tasks at home performed—his, the chopping of the wood and bringing up the cows and other chores ; and mine, the sewing and knitting and the washing of the dishes, with the cheery little mother in the lead. One by one three more dear ones came into the family, Effie and Isadora and Willie, and these in turn joined hands in the

happy home circle of willing and useful workers, trained
in hand and head and heart.

EDUCATION.

Younger and less spiritual preachers took the place of
the older itinerants, and with them new ideas sprang up
voicing the spirit of the more prosperous times of the
United States of America. Then the cry of '' Educate,
educate,'' ringing all along the line of the homesteads
in the Miami Valley, chimed in with the merry din and
rush of the farmer's toil ; and the two caused the morning and evening prayers at the home altar, with the
sacred melody of happy songs, to come irregularly. Alas !
Alas ! to my mother's sorrow. She took up afresh what
she had planned for us,—an education. Added to this,
the making of money, to my already prosperous father,
proved a snare ; and now the shadows were thrown
across the family hearth. Yet there was one, the patient,
loving mother, who stood firm to the principles of truth
and purity. My brother was sent to College Hill, Cincinnati, and I to Springfield Female College. Here vain
wisdom began to fill our minds. My brother had made
no profession of religion, but at nine years I became a
member of the Methodist Church and carried my letter
of probation to High Street M.-E. Church, next door
to the college, and soon was admitted and baptized by
sprinkling, by Brother John Marlay of the Cincinnati

Conference. By this time I was so cold, spiritually, that the dressing of my hair for the occasion seemed to quite fill my mind. O ! Those were dangerous days. However, the habits formed could not be quite lost sight of, and so I prayed nightly and in the morning, and read the word of God, and believed, intellectually at least, that I was a child of God—attending class and prayer meetings regularly, and speaking of truth but living it in works, and that very poorly I fear.

PRIDE

crept in. Soon I was longing to gratify my love of self and selfish adornments. More and more the worldly wisdom came in, and more and more the once simple and child-like faith went out. The music was delightful and improved in ; but the songs were not of the kind which could be sung in the name of the Lord, or the kind which thrilled my young heart ; yet I went on singing them all the same. And then when vacations came, and the piano and my brother's return with the violin in hand,—and he a skillful player,—O, then, with him, dear boy, it was the dance and society not in keeping with that of our dear parents' teaching. With me, though that was forbidden, yet other things as evil crept in ; and I was a cold and wandering girl, formal and superficial, proud of my face and attainments. In time the younger ones were sent off to grand schools, and all in a whirl we as a family were going back from God, as far as a real vital life was concerned; and dress and culture took the place of the dear simple faith of childhood's days. My heart aches as I write these things, and my memory falls upon other evils not to be written, as they are canceled by the precious blood of Christ. Hallelujah!

GOLD.

In the midst of this backsliding my father, with a company of worldly men, traveled overland to California in search of health and gold. These were trying days to my mother and her little ones. A house was built in the village near by, and there we lived until father's return.

Happily for us he was only away for one year; his speedy return being an experiment for life, as his physicians bade him return by water at once, as a remedy,— the last and only one they thought. By this time the lodge had claimed my father as a member,—this the first thing, perhaps, which made a way for him to be absent from his family at night. It led to sorer temptations, and the only redeeming feature of his membership in the Masonic order was reached as he left the wharf and entered the vessel which bore him down the Pacific and up the Atlantic to New York;—his brother Masons filled his pockets with gold.

Reports of his death often filled mother's heart with sorrow and her eyes with tears, but she took them with her little ones to God in prayer; and in a dream one night, thrice repeated, she was made certain of his return, which came to pass the following day, producing great joy to the reunited family. To our mother's memory be it said, that, whatever our waverings may have been, her trust in God never seemed to lag, and she ever professed her faith in Him both at home and in the meetings, yet often feeling and owning *our* disobedience and unfaithfulness.

THE COLLEGES.

Were they not Christian? O, yes! at least so-called; but the *real sins* and the *unreal* service, where could it end but in spiritual failure and certain success to Satan's kingdom, at least for the time being? To tell of the flirting of the presidents and the jealousy of their wives, which we at first doubted and afterward knew of, I would blush as much now to relate as I then feared to, and we children looking to them as our guides in spiritual things. Their preaching and reading at chapel service sadly lacked the sweet, sweet charm of the pure Gospel as heard and realized in the old log church. Where are you drifting? Answer the question in the light of God's blessed word and by the power of the Holy Ghost.

Christian parents, be careful how you send your children away from home. Mrs. Booth, in "Practical Religion," writes: "The training God requires is a moral training:

the inspiring of the child with the love of goodness,
truth and righteousness, and leading him to its practice
and exercise in all the duties and emergencies of life.
Now any parent can do this if only she has the grace
of God in her heart and will take the trouble. Training
a child in the way he shall go does not necessarily imply
a scholastic training.'' To my notion there is more
necessity of getting the *home righted* than any other
place in the world. There is more hope of succeeding in
moral and spiritual life according as parents obtain God's
grace, and then lead their children by their own responsible positions directly to God, they themselves making
the best use of the supreme influence God has given
them over their children. In modern schools there is,
to be sure, much truth, but it is so closely woven in
with error that scarcely one in a thousand can escape
the delusion, and prevent being engulfed sooner or later
in the most deathly moral corruption.

Our college days ended by my brother's craze for the
golden land and my utter repugnance of a wolf in
sheep's clothing,—the president of the Springfield Female
College.

MY TWO REQUESTS.

While a child I felt a desire to teach school when I
grew up; and if I ever married he should be a minister
of the gospel. These desires were realized. The first
vacation after I left the Springfield Female College I

returned one evening from the postoffice and found a strange gentleman in the parlor. Mother introduced him to me, "Sylvanus Hover of the M.-E. Church, just graduated from Delaware University, to be teacher in our school the coming year." At first I was not prepossessed in his favor, but strange to say, during the following winter, by an unusual Providence which had united us in friendship, we were fully launched on the sea of an all-absorbing love. He boarded at my father's house, and proved to be the most spiritual-minded man we had formed the acquaintance of for years. His influence was felt in our home, and the family altar was once more set up. He was then preparing for the ministry, and was soon after admitted in the North Indiana Conference, where he remained till sickness gave him a superannuated relation to that body. At or near the close of his school year with us we were walking in a lovely grove near by, and there we plighted our love, and knelt while he prayed God's blessing upon our engagement. Another year of teaching in the South, just at the beginning of the Civil war, brought to us our first sorrow. Our letters were intercepted. His politics were demanded, and he was commanded peremptorily to leave Kentucky, which he did in defense of his life. Another term of teaching and preparation and he was admitted ; and still two years passed by ere our vows were consummated by marriage. These were times of fidelity testing. I teaching in Ohio, Civil war raging, and the

long separation from one whom I have since learned to
know I loved more than I did the God to whom I daily
prayed, and of whom I constantly testified in the class
meetings. I desired and was seeking my Saviour, but
had allowed an idol to come between. The sin of this I
little dreamed of at the time, so absorbed was I with
thoughts of the absent loved one. In the mean time I
was working up a reputation as teacher in the common
schools, and in the Sunday school, and *seemed to be*
growing in grace,—so thought of by others.

Our Wedding.

On the 15th of April, 1862, a beautiful evening indeed, with all the loveliness of early spring-time, our
father's house was adorned and well supplied with wedding guests and wedding festivities. A loaded table in
the dining hall. Two happy pair stepped from an adjoining room into the center of a spacious parlor, and
Brother Robinson of the Cincinnati Conference pronounced Sylvanus Hover and Minnie H. Oakes man and
wife, all reverently kneeling in prayer. Congratulations
over, supper ended, and music preluded by " The Star
Spangled Banner" floated out on the ears of a merry
throng of loving friends. But alas ! The look of death
was there, and an old friend of our's, an aged lady,
saw it in the eyes and in the sunken chest of the young
husband, in whose lungs lay that latent dread disease,

consumption. The happy party took their loving fare-
wells, and the bridal party their tour to the new field of
labor, and soon were busy workers in the various churches
of New Paris circuit. These services on my part were so
heartless and formal as in these after years to cause me
to shudder on account of the spiritual danger I passed so
unconsciously at the time. During the first year the fell
typhoid laid my dear idol very low, and ten long weeks
of watching him with bated breath brought me down
also with the same malady. We were praying, and God
was answering by the only means—chastisement—which
could awaken or prepare us to know and live with Him.
We both slowly recovered, and the following summer our
home was brightened by the coming of a dear little son,
—Eddie,—who proved another idol for a few short
months, when the Father took him. In these later years
I understand that scene of death, as he lay in his little
crib at the midnight hour, after six weeks of painful
sickness, and just before he breathed his last looked
with bright and peaceful look of holy light round about
upon us all, each at a time,—a long look of loving farewell. It seemed strange and unaccountable to us at the
time for such seeming holy intelligence to take possession of a child; but some of that little circle have since
learned that it was the revelation to him—dear babe—of
the Holy Jesus, and a kingdom made pure within his
baby breast. Glory to God!

SCENES IN SCHOOL.

Soon after Eddie's death husband and I repaired to Rochester, Ind. He took the principalship of the Union School, being still in a superannuated relation to the conference, and I assisted. This was a hard field for weak and weary ones just out of such scenes of trial. The bad discipline of the school and the unruliness of some of the pupils can be illustrated by a scene of horror which neither of us had ever witnessed in our previous experience as teachers. My husband undertook to re-prove Scott Reynolds, who was a terror in the community, and the latter at once threw a rock and struck him on the temple, causing the blood to stream over his face. He was barely able to step to my door adjoining, and we had to retire to our room across the way, having dismissed for the time. The affair was soon settled by the expulsion of the young man. Such scenes were more than one breaking down in health could endure, and soon my dear husband was lain down with a complication of diseases. By his wish I took his place as principal, and conducted the school, putting an advanced pupil in my place. This however, with attending him in the intervals of teaching, was too much for me, and before four months of the school year had passed I, too, had resigned. From this time through the winter the tolling of the church bell near by was about the only music which greeted our ears, as typhoid carried away one or more out of many families. However, we escaped.

In the following June our dear mother came and took us home with her to Troy, Ohio, where

ANOTHER SCENE OF DEATH

ensued. In three weeks more of pain and sorrow he, too, my dear husband, left us to join little Eddie in Glory. He clung to life almost to the last, desiring to preach the Gospel he so much loved. Many had been the number "turned to righteousness" even in his short term of Christian labor, his first breaking down being in the midst of a blessed revival on New Paris circuit.

The Saturday before he died he called me to him where he sat in a rocker on the veranda in our dear old father's home, and said : "I have been unwilling to give you up *till now;* sing—

> " The dearest idol I have known,
> Whate'er that idol be,
> Help me to tear it from Thy throne,
> And worship only Thee."

With trembling voice and tearful eyes I complied ; and then he testified to me that all was surrendered, and he was resigned to go. The next Wednesday, being July 13th, he repeated with great difficulty part of the 23d Psalm, a dear friend finishing it for him. About 3 P. M. of that day, as friends were gathered about his bed, he motioned me to lean near him. He whispered : "Love the Lord ; trust in Jesus ;" and peacefully departed.

Oh ! the agony of that hour as I wrung my hands and wept. But soon, even that very night, I took hold of God by faith as never before. A sweet consolation came as I consecrated myself afresh to be the Lord's. As he lay prepared for burial the next evening I took a long look at his peaceful face, and said aloud, "We will meet again." This was my faith, praise God ! as my loved one was swept from my sight and lain in Rosehill Cemetery, Troy, Ohio. Our brother, Cornelius Hover, then of the same conference with us, but now of the Iowa Conference, joined us next day after the funeral, in time, at least, to share my sorrow and comfort my aching heart.

SORROW'S GLEANINGS.

To draw us to Him in closer embrace,
   The showers of sorrow fall,
"The light of his countenance" on our face,
   The storm cloud darkens for all.

But then we read on the sacred page,
   "He hath borne our sorrows" away ;
And now, while His words my thoughts engage,
   The darkness recedes,—'tis day.

There's light on ahead, I'll never turn back,
   But "believe to the saving of my soul ;"
Our Saviour leads on in this narrow track,
   And like Him I'll soon reach the goal.

O, Jesus, dear Jesus, pour the floods of glory down ;
   For I'll walk in the light, through sorrow's dark night,
And receive my starry crown.

Home Again.

My parents now for a time had removed from the farm and were living in Troy. I felt out of place, strange to say, and soon began arrangements to begin my chosen profession,—teaching. In the mean time working in the church, especially in prayer and Sunday school, the latter as teacher. My class of young ladies—dear to me—though only four in number, vying with the largest classes of older persons in giving missionary money, often getting in ahead at the last moment, after hearing reports from their classes. These were days of sore mourning for the two dear ones; and I failed of comfort in the various church socials. At this time my heart longed for more solid comfort. Indeed, I cannot remember the time when I did not possess a longing for something satisfying in the far-off distance. In a short time I repaired with a dear young friend, Nellie M. Gaylord, —afterward Mrs. Forbes, missionary to Africa,—to Pittsburg Female College to review and prepare for more advanced teaching. Never can I forget the keen sorrow which filled my heart as I once more found myself in school as a pupil with ladies mostly younger than myself. Oh! the agony as the reality of hopes so suddenly blighted took hold upon me. It was too deep for tears; and a sadness too palpable to deny stole over every feature of my countenance, which at times wrought for me a deep sympathy from the most careless and unconcerned. We two, Nellie and I, were seeking spiritual

3

blessings as well as the fading wisdom of this world, and together we sought the Saviour in prayer, the study of the word, attending all the means of grace at Christ M.-E. Church. Soon we were requested to take classes at Prospect Mission Sunday School, which we did, having in our classes children living in "dug-outs." They seemed wild and unruly; but soon the sweet salvation songs quelled them into calmness, as a dear little converted Jew brought melody from the organ. A flourishing school we had, and all seemed so happy sitting in the pretty camp stools in the lovely little mission church on Prospect Hill every Sunday afternoon, with Florence Cramer, a wealthy banker of Pittsburg, acting as superintendent. I can yet almost hear his commanding tones calling out to "Sue," a member of my class, to bring her to order, when she was bent on removing my furs that she might the better examine them. However, our many "works of righteousness" were destitute of a charm, I have since found. Hallelujah! I often wondered, as I read the joy depicted in the Bible,—the joy of God's children,—what could be the matter with us all; and a deep sadness sunk my heart lower and lower in disappointment. Our order for the week was very systematic, of course. On Sunday, chapel service in college first thing; prayers in dining hall next, class at Christ Church following; preaching at 11 A. M. O, such grand sermons, with artistic singing and pipe organ. Afternoon Sunday school at the mission; then S. S. at Christ

Church ; then prayer meeting in chapel, and preaching at the church at night. O, what weary bodies and minds we had on Monday morning. "The way of the transgressor is hard." On Wednesday night prayer meeting in the college, and the whole week the weary routine of studies and recitations. My life was somewhat varied, as I was often appointed monitor, or teacher, to fill some one's place, or to escort young ladies out in the city, etc. The Holy Spirit evidently led dear Nellie and I in one heart and in one way. We were daily learning to

"Cease to do evil and learn to do well."

We were in harmony always, and held together in love, aiding each other. When evil reports came to us of the undue familiarity of Pres. P——, we would not believe it until we saw for ourselves, and then our hearts were pained beyond measure, as we had raised a *very high* standard of character for one in so responsible a place. From that time we avoided him, which he seemed to feel keenly.

As the old scenes of evil "flirtations" presented them-selves as before at Springfield College, my very heart revolted ; but, as before, I neither had power nor courage to either report the offender or to speak directly to him of his sin. These things soon discouraged me from remain-ing, especially as a dear teacher resigned on account of these things, and some young ladies were taken away from the institution. Having stayed some two years I was requested to take the position of preceptress of New

Carlisle Academy in Indiana, while my dear room-mate
Nellie taught in a school in Pennsylvania.   At this time
I was in constant reception of some very devoted letters
from an M. D. in Indiana, who stood high in medical
circles and was very wealthy.   I could not accept him
for two reasons : I did not love him, and

He Was Not a Christian.

Furthermore, I had made up my mind not to marry, as
my memory clung to the dear one so ruthlessly torn from
me ; thus I continued ever to brood over the sorrow of my
young life.   But, *at this writing*, will you please listen to
the song of my happy heart ?   It is this, dear reader :

> "I'm satisfied with Jesus here.
>   He's everything to me ;
>   His dying love has won my heart,
>   And now He sets me free."

I am so glad of the privilege of singing this little testimony right here.   Hallelujah !

A part of the year I taught in the school named with
success, but as the attendance was small, and it was sup-
ported by tuition fund alone, I was obliged to resign,
having been using my own means to support me.

Another Wedding

called me to Troy, where my dear sister—now, I trust, in
Heaven—was married to Lieutenant Ashworth.   From

there I visited sister Isadora, then in Xenia College, for
a few months, as a parlor boarder, taking a course of
music. Here I found my sorrow, at least outwardly,
wearing away, and an undercurrent of *vanity* and *selfish
love* stealing down deep within me; and I soon left the
fashionable society into which I was brought and took
the principalship of Union School, in Addison, Ohio,
where I remained as teacher for one year; and so on I
continued to teach for a space of time running about
twenty years in all, ever having a "profession" of religion,
and, as it were, a "hope" only of Heaven beyond this
world. The forms were strictly adhered to : the strict
life, carrying my Church certificate from place to place,
as my pastor said it would help me in many ways tem-
porally to do so. I can now look back and see the decep-
tion which to me then seemed right enough. Satan will

"Deceive the very elect"

if possible. Beware of this "deceiving and being deceived." It is too dangerous to be tampered with.
These are now the "perilous times" spoken of by the
apostle. O, take warning, my dear reader, and "flee
the wrath to come." The history of my blessed release
and escape will come later on. Be patient.

About this time a latent hereditary foe, fanned into
flame by many errors of life, dress and neglect, made its
appearance in the form of deafness, which unfitted me
for duty as a teacher. Thank God ! this was a blessing

in disguise, which led me to my dear mother and the dear
old homestead where my parents at the time were living, with one colored servant. It was evident that dear
mother's health was declining, and I was detailed as
mistress of the house. Financial troubles, which family
pride and gratification had brought on, injured dear
father's business capacity, and involved the estate in
danger if not overthrow. My brother Samuel, who had
made frequent visits from his California home, had once
more returned. At this time a brother-in-law became
involved, and, as father's business failures were not gen-
erally known, his name on a note was gladly accepted
by a party to whom brother-in-law was indebted. At
this time the remaining property had been transferred
to my brother. This led to great trial, especially to dear
mother and I, whose conscience revolted at such measures. We heartily expostulated with father and brother
to no avail. The whole family seemed wrecked finan-
cially, and honesty held in jeopardy, with the usual train
of misery in such cases. O, how sad mother and I were.
We had lived ahead of our means, and unhappiness was
the result. For two long, lonely years the farm-work
slowly proceeded with little income. Mother's health,
through sorrow, still declining, and my nerves, with the
cares and disappointments, fairly shattered. The old
piano held its place in the large, old-fashioned parlor,
hardly ever opened by me. The loud "Burdett" organ
took its place in the worship, and in this way many a

sorrow took its flight for the time, as with self-abandon-
ment I poured out my soul to God in holy song, longing
for the power of those words of praise to God ; while my
dear old parents, loving the solemn strains, gathered
near me in the eventide and sang with heavy hearts as
the loneliness of old age crept over them :

> " Behold the record, Lord and see,
> If I have lived this day for Thee,
> And where I fail, O, pardon me !
> O, pardon me ! O, pardon me !''

Thinking dear mother would be benefited by a journey she was prepared and took a trip to Indiana, accompanied by myself a part of the way. She spent some
weeks very delightfully with her sister Matilda, near
where dear sister Isadora was at her life-work—music
teaching—since her graduation from Xenia Female College. At the close of the visit dear sister returned home
with mother, and spent most of the time of the remaining
year of dear mother's life with us at home. This brightened up the old home some, as company came, and sister
was more happy in the world, and spent much time
driving her own horse, given by father, in which pastime
she took delight, sometimes getting dear mother and I
to share her favorite recreation, often to our fears, as
"Bessie," the little black mare, took spells of jumping
to one side very suddenly, my sister only enjoying such
freaks, priding herself in horsemanship. A party of

friends surprised us occasionally, or we were invited out
to similar places of social resort, and in this way the
time dragged on. We attended worship on Sundays in
the village near by. O, the formality of the worship!
Did every one feel it as we did, I wonder! I doubt it.
My dear mother and I were dying out, and held some
sweet consultations, and she assured me my seeking our
Saviour was becoming more real and apparent to all.
Our Bibles were well worn, and the prayers morning,
noon and night, and all along in between, became our
chief delight and comfort, as at the throne of grace, in
the large old wardrobe on the second floor, we poured
out our souls to God. Dear father was tried, quiet and
weak, but often drove out, and sometimes worked a little
on the farm, of which brother had charge. The pastimes
of the latter were chiefly the violin (with which he had
kept time for many a dance party on the Pacific Coast),
accompanied by sister Isadora on piano, or dear brother
Willie, who had married a sweet singer, and was sometimes found visiting at the old farm; and he, Willie,
would bring up his part on cornet, or bass-viol, while a
neighbor boy fond of the art brought up some pleasant
part on another instrument. Sometimes when we returned from church the instruments were all going in
regular orchestral style; and many were the chidings
dear brother received from us, as we contended for the
sanctity of the Sabbath, all in vain. The influence of
his Western life of freedom seemed to harden his heart to

all those tender associations which clustered around his early life at home.

The Dark Clouds Were Gathering.

One Saturday night, just after dear brother had left us for California, with only father, mother, sister Isadora and I at home, dear mother fell sick at once—dangerously ill. And without the doctor's aid, I, who was her constant attendant (Isadora and father doing the work), diagnosed that awful malady, typhoid, and knew my mother could not rally in her weak state. I was driven almost to distraction. The conflict with me was short and sharp. I went to God and had a little talk with Him. I besought Him to reconcile me, and prepare me with strength, which, praise His dear name, He did at once; so that with steady, firm and unflinching movement I went forward ministering to her in this time of pain and anguish. A dear Christian doctor, our friend, did all in his power by prayer and by medicine. All possible attention was given, even to the muffling of the door-bell, that she might be kept quiet. The fever raged, and at times she begged to be taken to the cool spring at the foot of the hill upon which the house stood ; or, perhaps, for a time her mind wandered. O, what days of painful sick-room scenes were these ! But Jesus, dear Jesus, was there, and some hearts by naked faith took in that rich blessing of His presence, and built upon the

rock. The following Sabbath, dear mother feeling better,
father and sister left us long enough to attend morning
service ; and during this time the Angel of the Lord en-
compassed dear mother and I as I read to her just where
she had left off in her Bible, "The wise woman buildeth
her house ;" and we felt sweetly assured that the Lord
had builded for her, and we were comforted. The next
night, during severe pain, I repeated to her these words,
"Now faith is the substance of things hoped for, the
evidence of things not seen." She from that time took a
firmer hold upon God, and thus we prayed and trusted
together. On the same evening she said to sister and I,
"Sing." Isadora seated herself at the organ in sight
of dear mother from the adjoining room where she
lay, and we opened on the dear hymn, "I am trusting
Lord in Thee," and sang it through ; and at the closing
verse,—

> "Jesus comes; He fills my soul;
>   Perfected in love I am;
> I am every whit made whole;
>   Glory, Glory to the Lamb."

we looked toward her to see her raised up in bed, and
smiling the most peaceful smile of victory and joy we had
ever seen upon the face of a trusting child of God. She
lay back upon her pillow and rested, and at midnight her
holy joy had increased until her face shown with holy
light too deep for our understanding at the time; but as
we looked wonderingly upon her, and then at each other,

we knew it was the blessing of God, and felt a precious
sympathy of love to Him and to our dear, departing
mother. On and on we ministered night and day,
until óne evening the doctor bade me go to my room
and rest for the night, or "I would not be able to attend
mother any more. I obeyed, taking a dose of "nervine"
which he ordered, and thus was enabled to be with her
to the last. The day before she died, dear sister Effie,
with her sweet little girl Pearlie, came from a distant
State just in time to spend a day and night with mother.
She looked her recognition with pleasant and restful
smiles, unable to say anything. During her sickness she
called at times, Oh! so longingly, for "father," and was
satisfied when he came to her bedside, but sometimes
said sorrowfully, "Why did you do so?" We thought
she referred to financial interests, and was grieved to leave
things so, as the estate came by her. Dear father felt it
keenly, no doubt; but the bitter cup he too soon was also
to drink. The last evening friends were gathered and
sang sweet notes of salvation, and I comforted her till the
last, reminding her of what our dear Saviour had borne
for her, and exhorted her to the patient endurance unto
the end. Slowly and shortly came the breath until Sunday morning about day-dawn, and the freed soul plumed
its wings and soared away to dwell with God. This was
September 17, 1876. This was the last I remembered,
and friends bore me from a sofa where I sank down, raging with typhoid fever, to my room above. Only one

scene do I remember till the crisis was passed.   A friend
raised me up in bed, put a shawl around me, and I
looked at my side and saw for the last time my beautiful
mother in a robe of white in her casket.   The tuberoses
filled the room with their perfume, and the pall-bearers
with the white crape stood at my feet.   This lasted but a
moment, but stamped a never to be forgotten memory.
It seemed a forerunner of a pure and never-ending meeting for dear mother and I in the realm beyond.   My life
hung on a thread.   All friends.had despaired, and my
dear Doctor Hartman prayed, and owned at last

It was the Prayer of Faith

that saved me.   How kind he was to me ; and how they
cheered my heart, the doctor, my sister Isadora and dear
Anna Ripley, as they stood by my bedside the hour I
came to consciousness and sang:

> "Ring the bells of Heaven; there is joy to-day,
>   For a soul returning from the wild.
> See, the Father meets her out upon the way,
>   Welcoming His own belovèd child.
> Glory! Glory! how the angels sing ;
>   Glory! Glory! how the old harps ring.
> 'Tis the ransomed army, like a mighty sea,
> Pealing forth the anthem of the free."

This was a prelude to the dear life coming, and a result
and answer to prayer,—my prayer and promise to God as

I lay there that I would work for Him if He restored me, and I shouted aloud the praises of God. As the sickness had been short and dreadful, so the convalescence was slow and painful.

Dear brother, who came the day of mother's death, remained with us; and, when they thought a change of scene would do me good, he, though himself weak from sickness and sorrow at the loss of dear mother, took me in his arms and carried me to a room on the first floor. And there, where I could see all,—but the one dearest of all,—my heart broke. I had always thought this would be the greatest trial of my life, and it was up to that time. Here, for the first time, I realized fully my mother's absence, and a sadness too deep for tears took hold of my heart. It seemed my heart was expanding and pressing out of the membrane which surrounded it, and my loud groans brought every one within hearing to my bed. They *saw what it was.* And first one and then another tried to comfort me, and failed, until I thought I, too, should die. Then dear Willie took me in his arms, and with tears and words of solace touched my heart. My tears streamed down, bringing the needed relief. Thank God !

They were all very kind to me, and a young friend, Preston Miller, came in often and sang and played on my favorite instrument, the organ, which they had rolled into my room for this purpose. Often I joined him, as my faith took hold, and though not seeing,

yet believing, I poured out my soul in praise to God,
singing:

> "Come to the light, 'tis shining for thee ;
> Sweetly the light hath dawned upon me ;
> Once I was blind, but now I can see.
> The light of the world is Jesus."

Still my sorrow seemed unabated, only when the doctor
came in and spoke so sweetly of the way of faith in
Jesus.   My faith for *my own personal salvation* seemed to
be *prospective* rather than a *present reality*.   I know *now*
that this was my greatest lack ; but I know, too, that at
the time I little realized the truth of the matter.

A PRESENTIMENT.

One afternoon, being left alone, I thought I would try
to drag my weak limbs to the parlor, where my organ
then stood.   It was difficult work.   By taking hold of a
chair or door-knob or table, or anything, in fact, along
the way, I helped myself to the seat, sat down and leaned
my head on the music-board till I rested ; then I opened
on a new piece in the Gospel Hymns,—

> "Not now, my child,"

and read it over with the music, and felt that God gave
it to me, and that it was to be fulfilled in my life in
answer to my promise to work for God with entire

consecration if he healed me. That song which I then sang for the first time has been fulfilled in me with

A GLORIOUS FULFILLMENT,

and for that reason I give a copy of it below :

"Not now, my child, a little more rough tossing,
  A little longer on the billows' foam ;
A few more journeyings in the desert darkness,
  And then the sunshine of thy Father's home.

Not now, for I have wanderers in the distance,
  And thou must call them in with patient love ;
Not now, for I have sheep upon the mountains,
  And thou must follow them where'er they rove.

Not now, for I have loved ones, sad and weary ;
  Wilt thou not cheer them with a kindly smile ?
Sick ones who need thee in their lonely sorrow,—
  Wilt thou not tend them yet a little while ?

Not now, for wounded hearts are sorely bleeding,
  And thou must teach those widowed hearts to sing ;
Not now, for orphans' tears are quickly falling,
  They must be gathered 'neath some sheltering wing.

Go with the name of Jesus to the dying,
  And speak that name in all its living power ;
Why should thy fainting heart grow chill and weary ?
  Canst thou not watch with Him one little hour ?

One little hour, and then the glorious crowning,
  The golden harp-strings and the victor's palm ;
One little hour, and then the hallelujah !—
  Eternity's long, deep thanksgiving psalm."

Seeking Opportunity to Do Good.

As my strength came back again I sought and found many ways to speak or act or look for God and humanity. This was my chief thought,—how I might accomplish this one absorbing desire. At this time I formed the acquaintance of a spiritually minded family by the name of Little, and with them attended the meetings, seeking to win souls to Christ. With them many an hour was spent in singing praise to God. How I loved these associations. Some of these have since sought and testified to the finding of pure hearts through *faith in the*

Atonement

of our dear Saviour. My desire to do something often manifested itself in feeding a tramp, or singing a song of salvation to him or to some weary Jew peddler. The dear songs so touched my own heart that I longed to reach other sad, lonely and afflicted ones, and especially the poor, in this way. I cannot remember a time in my childhood when I did not have an innate sympathy and deep pity for the down-trodden. Brother Samuel and I, when the anti-slavery question was at its height, often discussed with great enthusiasm the joy that it would give us to have enough money to buy up every slave south of Mason and Dixon's line and then set them free. My convalescence was so slow that I could do but little rugged toil for some months. In the mean time dear father, who had so kindly attended me during my sickness, fell a prey to

PNEUMONIA.

At first it assumed so mild a form we were not alarmed, but suddenly it assumed a fatal form, and he, too, was taken away from us in the most extreme winter weather. How earnestly I besought the Lord to prepare him for what so surely seemed to await him. My faith rested peacefully in Jesus for the answer, as our dear father sunk into the cold embrace of death. Until the last he requested us to sing the sweet hymns of praise. Once, when we were both well, I had requested him to sing for me if I went first; but now it proved to be my work to ask them to sing for him when dying. Oh! how sorrowful were the group of children present,—all but Samuel, who was then in the far West. We all knelt around his bed, and some friends sang, "The angels are hovering 'round;" and our dear father signaled to us that all was well with his soul, and, as we breathed amen to a prayer offered up for him by Brother Little his spirit took its flight to God. He was prepared for burial, so sweetly, as was dear mother,—the cross and anchor of pure flowers, with his name and age on a silver plate on the casket; and he too was lain in our lot in Rosehill cemetery. Brother Willie and I each had presentiments of more sorrow soon to come, as we rode in the carriage together to dear father's funeral. Was any family ever so oppressed? Let the suffering, sorrowing families of fallen humanity answer truly, and *each will answer—yes!*

FINANCIAL TROUBLE.

Soon after father's death brother Samuel returned from California, desiring to settle up the estate; and for this purpose he advertised extensively the sale of real estate, and a large list of stock, household goods, etc. This brought together on the day appointed a vast number of people. But no sooner had the auctioneer taken his stand than the sheriff called him down, and all was attached for the note referred to before. The holder of it knew at the time that he could do nothing, as the law sustained our brother; but he was rich and wanted to take revenge, and was willing to pay for it. When the sheriff came into the house and spoke to sisters and I about it, our feelings of embarrassment were simply crushing, and the open disgrace fearful. The sheriff,—what did he care? Where was his sympathy, as with cool and amused indifference he made his statements? The crowd in the mean time was swiftly dispersing,—no one a word of sympathy. All seemed surprised, too much so to speak.

"Earth knows no sorrow that Heaven cannot cure;" and strange as it seemed to all, even to dear Dr. Hartman, who was standing near the front entrance, I seated myself at the organ, and with an intense longing

to help some poor soul to a better life began singing an
all-victorious salvation melody. So unusual was this
that soon the word rang round, "She has been sick, and
her mind is wandering." "Is she right?" I think the
dear angel of the covenant, our dear Jesus, would have
said : "Yes ; my child's mind is wandering up to me ;
and by my blood, shed for her, she will soon be right."
My happiness even then at times, though transient, of
course, was grand, as my heart's hope took hold of God
by faith ; and my blessed anticipation of a better time
coming brought sweet relief from the outward strife of
that hour. My dear brother, after this scene, remarked
to us privately that it was well for the man who stopped
that sale that he did not see him, or, indeed, know that
he was on the ground, as he was armed in California
fashion. But God, who is so merciful to his poor, dis-
obedient people, spared us such a scene of horror as might
have ensued. My health at this time was only recover-
ing ; but soon after I began work by teaching music,
and sewing some, feeling very weary when night came.
When daily, from my window, I saw the minister, my
pastor, and his family taking seats in their lovely
phaeton for their accustomed ride, I would think, "Oh,
how I long for them to call upon me and offer sympathy
in my lonely sorrow and sickness and toil !" I wondered why they did not, and a feeling of condemnation
would rise up within me. *I know now why they did not,*
and O, so freely, forgive them.

COMING EVENTS

were speedily revealed as their dark shadows had been cast about our hearts. Every effort to sell failed, and my brother returned to the Coast. Soon after, to my astonishment, there came to me from him a warranty deed to the entire estate, made by law so strong that nothing could take away my title. This was *law*, and in the sight of men legal ; but to me it seemed simply dreadful, and that night I lay awake and wept. And after tampering with the convictions I left the deed at the Recorder's office to be recorded, and employed a real estate agent, and soon a buyer came to me, after my dear old Aunt Rachael had told him that "What I said I would do, he might depend upon it." The transfer was made, and the proper share of each heir was promptly set out as my brother and the family had agreed upon during my sickness. Once more we were at rest. My brother, subsequent to the attempted sale, had filed a bill for the quieting of the title, which was granted him at a great expense of money and mind. In the mean time he had married, and in due time a little girl was given him ; and her little heart, the heart of Minnie Rose, and her papa, were knit together in a strange, deep love for an infant and a man past the prime of life. The mother failed of an abiding affection and that tender solicitude which mostly characterizes, or should characterize, the affections of one in such a relation. My brother felt this sorely, and at once made known his desires to me to come and have the care of the little one so precious to his heart. Time and again he wrote to this effect. I saw many impediments in the way, but most of all dreaded to leave the society of my staid old State, Ohio, and come upon the fast and reckless scenes of the Western coast. My previous kindness to him, myself preparing his wedding feast and entertainment, and presiding over the home when he had it in charge, and in adjusting his business so satisfactorily to him, added to the fact of loaning him a nice sum of several hundred, all of which involved much care, labor and trouble of mind, seemed to bind me to him; and he depended upon me instead of his Saviour; and soon following upon the former events there came to me one day, where I was visiting a friend,

ANOTHER STARTLING EVENT.

Taking out my mail from the postoffice I observed an official document. It was another warranty deed from my brother made as solid as the rock of law could make it, to a valuable piece of real estate in Nevada. I was shocked, surprised and sad, knowing full well by past experience where such measures would end. A few more days and nights of weeping for me were speedily followed by still more awful deep and heartrending sorrow. This last document I received was followed by a dispatch in a few days announcing the

Murder of Our Dear Brother Samuel.

My brother-in-law read the news to dear sister Effie and I. She was in the act of cutting out a garment, and I sat at leisure near her. When the shock rolled over our hearts, each of us instinctively clasped our hands about them as if to stop their bounding, breaking power. Oh! such grief. Sister was in a delicate state of health. Premature sickness was the result. For six weeks I watched with her, determining as soon as her recovery to go to the scene of sorrow, and comply with my brother's long-cherished desire for me to care for and educate his child, and, if possible, also to comfort the widow. Every night we wept ourselves to sleep. This, to our remaining family, seemed the hardest of all the very hard blows endured. When nearly a week had passed, a long, sad and extremely grievous letter, on Thanksgiving day, explaining the case, reached us, and was read with breathless interest. A good deal of mystery then and yet hangs about the affair, but this was the statement received: On Saturday night brother was away from his home at his accustomed work, orchestral playing, and returning home found the little one sick, as was often the case. On Sunday evening he watched with her, and growing restless started for a doctor, saying, "I will be back in half an hour." Not finding the doctor in his office he started for his residence. His knocks at the door not bringing any one to him he called out for the doctor.

The doctor's wife being alone was frightened and fired a
revolver through the door. He was hard of hearing,
and she stated that she had requested him to go away.
This to some seemed plausible, but not those who had
seen his worst known enemy follow him in the direction
of Dr. S——'s. However, I leave these sorrowful and
sinful scenes for eternity to reveal, if the Lord in His
goodness does not reveal them sooner. What bore me
up as with a mighty power *was this*: Just at that fatal
hour I was in my room two thousand miles away pouring out my soul to God in prayer for that brother, and by
a neighbor near the scene he was heard in his dying
throes to be calling upon God. This to me—this hope of
a saved brother calling upon the Lord for himself and his
dear little one—gave me a blessed relief which took away
the sting. My dear brother was found by a night watch-
man a few rods from where the deed was supposed to
have been done, —found having been in a kneeling
position. He was borne to the morgue, and from there
to his home, and the next day the funeral, through dear
brother Willie's plan, took place from the M.-E. Church.
Near Laurel Avenue a hand upon his tombstone points
toward heaven, where sometime soon I hope to see dear
brother ; and, as sure as our Father through Jesus' name
hears and answers the prayer of faith, my hope is well
grounded. Praise the Lord ! To our dear brother
Willie living in the place this was an awful blow. He
was declining in health, and his wife an invalid ; but our

merciful Saviour whom he sought in childhood was very kind to him and sent him means and comfort.

Effie's Recovery

once effected, I was soon in readiness for my journey to the town of Reno, where these recent scenes had taken place. Bidding dear Effie, who stood in the door with tearful eye, a loving farewell, some dear friends met me at the train, and my brother-in-law accompanied me to the nearest city. Passing through Indianapolis, near where sister Isadora was teaching, I took a lay-over check and visited her for a day and night. This gave each one of us a sweet pleasure. In Council Bluffs I stopped once more till the west-bound train made up, and visited briefly a nephew and family of my dear Sylvanus. This, too, afforded great relief on such a mission. They bade me God speed, loading me down with good things, when dear Sanford took me again to my train. Cold and dreary was the journey over the desert and plains and table land against high head winds. But every comfort and available blessing was mine. The blessed Word of God which I read daily, and hope through him, gave a new zest to this strange work of Providence.

At times I was quite contented. A family of gold-miners from California returning from Europe were very kind to me, and all the more so as my nephew had

related to them my recent affliction and the occasion of
my tour. Very pleasant was our intercourse. They were
not Christians, but seemed sober, moral and refined.
We were constant companions, the lady and I, and
formed a sweet friendship which led to a promise to cor-
respond. They attended me to the last, till Reno was
reached, when they escorted me to a waiting-room in the
depot, and bidding me good-by boarded their train.
How fearful was this waiting in a sitting-room adjoining a saloon full of drunken men, asleep or awake. At
2 A. M. my brother Willie, to whom I had wired, came
for me. O, the mingled joy and sadness of that meeting,
—my joy through the hope in Jesus, and meeting him,
and his joy at seeing me, and the recent arrival of a
dear little boy, Paul, a few days previous, and our
mutual sorrow in the loss of our brother in that terrible
manner.

SORROWING AND REJOICING

is not only given to the saints in all the fullness of God,
but in all the forms of life the sweet and the bitter seem
to go together, either alternating or blending in one. I
arrived just in time for a lovely Christmas dinner and
reception given us by a cousin living in the place.
There I met my sister-in-law for the third time, having
seen her for a few hours at a time twice before. It was
then I saw my dear little niece, my brother's only child,

Minnie, for the first time. My sister-in-law and I at once took rented rooms, for she had sold her home my brother had just before his death deeded to her. "Be not unequally yoked together with unbelievers," was a command I soon found myself to be disobeying. Each day brought fresh trials from this cause. My zeal for the sister and the child continued until it seemed altogether impracticable for me to remain with them. For nine months they were my constant care to do them good, bearing many burdens of toil.

My brother being indebted to me in some ways I made up my mind to accept the property, as it was his purpose to see me paid, and he had made the transfer of his own free will without my knowledge. I allowed her as administratrix to offer it for sale, intending to deal honestly, paying off all his debts if possible, and using the rest for sister and Minnie's good as well as for my own. I did not dream but this could be done easily enough. But soon, alas! I found her associations so different from those I desired that we daily grew *apart* instead of *together*. Her course of conduct toward me in various dealings caused me in discouragement to give up morning and evening worship with her. Thenceforward my prayers were in secret. Daily, however, I poured out my soul in holy song, and the music of the sweet-toned instrument I had rented made our home pleasanter by far. Reports of advantage taken, and the unmistakable truth of these tales, filled me with sorrowful apprehension of where these things would end, but with a zeal born of heaven I endured,—

PRAYING WITHOUT CEASING.

One day sister wanted to go out and take the child in the cab. The little one, who always loved the very sight of her little carriage, cried and seemed sick. It was a very bad day. I begged her not to take her out, to which she complied. I then went off to my work, and soon observed that she had taken her out in the windstorm, returning with a very sick child. The doctor next door was consulted, and thought nothing much ailed her. I treated her as he directed, and the next day when the doctor called again little Minnie was in a comatose state. The doctor trembled as he bent over the little crib. I asked him if I could sponge her off. He said, "Do anything you want to." I took the dear little thing to God; and without further consultation with the doctor or any one else she was soon out of danger, and returning to a comfortable state of health, her mother looking on afar off during these scenes of watching and ministering. In ten short months there seemed every indication that she was planning to marry. This surprised and grieved me beyond measure on account of the person in view. He had just come upon the scene from the capital, where he had been confined for some time previous for wife-slaughter. This seemed

the affinity. Friends came and advised, begging for
little Minnie's sake if for no other, but to no avail.
About the time of these revelations, my deed, the
primary having been relinquished to the lawyer acting.
for the administratrix and for me also. I found that I
was being deceived in the whole scheme, both by the
lawyer and his client. This was very aggravating, as I
had since my arrival paid off with my last money over
eleven hundred dollars, taking off a mortgage on the
estate, thus relieving it of all embarrassment. My defect
in hearing gave cause for anxiety also, this blocking up
my way for teaching. About this time I remembered
the invitation of my California friends to come and visit
them. I wrote to them accordingly, though the estate
was far from being settled. Before starting I procured
the services of another lawyer, contracting for a certain
price with him to see that my right was obtained. Just
before the day appointed for the sale of the property I
received a telegram from my lawyer stating that *he was
not well*, and could not attend the sale the next day at
one o'clock. All this time I was leaving the matter to
God,—*to decide for me* according to His will, yet feeling
justified in making an effort to at least save something
for my own needs. During a conversation with my
lawyer just before leaving for California, when I asked
how I should be sure that she would pay me the money
due me at the sale of the property, he frankly replied,
''You could appoint some one to go and bid it in *for you*

if you wanted to." At once I spoke to the dear friend I was visiting, and told her I was in trouble. She sent for a neighbor attorney. Briefly, but definitely, I stated the facts to him. He advised me to at once wire to some friend, if I had such in the place, to buy it in for me at the exact value, not more or less. I did so, and the next day my cousin dispatched to me saying,—

"THE PROPERTY IS YOURS."

At the moment the operator came to my door to deliver this message I was on my knees begging God to withhold it or give it freely as was His will, feeling sure He was able and willing to provide for me. Even in those days I could not but submit everything to Him, beseech-Him to *make me submit* and fully trust Him. In a few days I received a letter full of wrath, but still I desired to do them good with all the means available. For this purpose I returned at once to Reno One thing remained to be done. The public administrator had to give his signature to the transaction, as her marriage, which had already taken place, cut off her power to act further in the case.

INTERVIEW WITH MY ATTORNEY.

He knew not what to do ; but, with a firm blow of his fist upon the desk, he said, "I know who is doing this now, and if this is not settled for you it will be because it can't be done." And it was, in a few days more. My trial during these scenes was extreme. At times, while trying to pray, as I never once gave up this form of worship, it seemed I should despair instead of trust.

To get to see my brother's child was denied me. Various threats came instead. I suffered much. Whatever had been my sins I had hitherto been untrammeled by such relationships and such transactions. Being outwardly honest from habitual training, and by honest toil loving my chosen life-work, and faithfully following it up, each day committing myself to the Lord for guidance and blessing, my journals written even in my school days bearing me witness.

WEDLOCK.

During my stay in California, which far transcended anything I had ever witnessed before in majesty of scenery, beauties of travel and hospitality of entertainment, I formed the acquaintance of one who proved a friend in need. This friend was Francis M. Peck, of Yuba County. His life had been the opposite of mine in opposite forms. He had been devoted to the dance and other worldly influences which I had escaped. When he made the proposition of marriage I was much surprised, not being accustomed to California style. I told him frankly I could not marry one not a Christian. He then stated his weariness of the life he led, and had long desired to be a Christian, which he fully intended to do. This changed the matter, and with his promise to join the people of God we plighted our faith to unite our fortunes for life. A ring was placed upon my finger, and as soon as my business in Reno was completed I journeyed to Nevada City, California, where I rested at the International Hotel for one week. He then joined me there, and on that very day, February 21, 1881, at the Methodist parsonage, Brother Jonathan L. Mann, of the California Conference, performed the ceremony which made us man and wife.

THE VIEW OF ROSES.

Once .before leaving my native State for the Pacific Coast I had a dream which I related next day to our pastor's wife. I saw in the sky millions of roses. The sky was everywhere full of them,—roses in full bloom. All at once they took the form of wreaths, until the whole expanse above was literally filled with wreaths of blooming beauty. My California and Nevada experience seemed a real fulfillment of this dream, constantly intensifying as the days passed by. The power was from above, from our Father in heaven. He went before His child who earnestly sought Him, never giving it up in discouragement.

Our wedding tour lay over the Sierra and down the ravines, along the vines and flowers which even then were springing up in lovely forms of beauty, and under the sunny skies which shed a halo of glowing light, indicative of future good. Our span of horses, used to mountain journeys, made the time in haste. After resting over the first evening at San Juan, we reached the village of Camptonville, which was to be our home for the time being. After dinner at the hotel, once owned as a partner by my husband, we walked around the square to his home in the suburbs, being a pretty ranch, with flowers and fields and gardens and fruits of lovely variety, hue and flavor. An order from the grocery, the neat and clean pantry was supplied ; and, after a cozy little supper was over, we merely looked in upon a company of friends who were at Army Hall making merry on Washington's birthday. This was our last in such scenes. My husband vowed it could not be the world and the Lord too. We started out for life to seek

HOLINESS UNTO THE LORD.

The dear old Bible was taken up by my new friend, and one of Isaiah's beautiful pen pictures presented to our minds, as with charming voice he read ; and then we knelt for the first time in such relations, and fervently besought the Saviour to bless us together and make us of one heart and mind. We were deeply in earnest, hence Satan was roused from his lair and made the conflict a hot one ; but, thank God, at this writing victory perches upon our banners, and we are running up the shining way.

BATTLES FOR ETERNAL LIFE.

The merry mountaineers sadly missed their comrade and my pleasant comminglings in their social ways, and some of them fought us. We took a firm stand for temperance, refusing the wine cup so often proffered in this land of the lovely grape. My husband's ambition was to be a temperance lecturer and a Christian of the highest type. This desire was partially realized when he delivered in our village some original lectures on the subject, which made them open their eyes, and which brought to me one day a saloon-keeper's wife with threats. "It was my fault," she said, and "we were ruining her husband's business, and he was old and unable to work." Well for her that she made her exit just before my husband's return. I fear he would have fallen from grace long enough to give her trouble. We were members of the I. O. G. T. The loose manner in which it was conducted brought forth our severe criticism, and all the more when some favorite of society was permitted to hold his membership and still go on drinking. They heeded not our entreaties for reverence when the chaplain performed her service, and after waiting patiently for awhile we quietly withdrew.

JOINING THE CHURCH.

Brother Hazen, of the California Conference, made occasional visits to the village to preach. Upon one of these occasions he admitted my husband into the Methodist ranks. Seeing his zeal and earnest search after a good life, felt that he should preach. To this end he gave him a copy of Wesley's sermons, requesting him to read one on Sunday. He complied, taking the text, " Awake, thou that sleepest, and arise from the dead, and Christ shall give thee light." Reverently he conducted the meeting while some of his former friends sat on the back seat making fun. From this time he was brought into service on funeral and other occasions when no minister was at hand.

SUNDAY SCHOOL.

My delight ran high with every promotion of my husband in good works. So when he was called to the superintendency of the Camptonville Sunday School, and myself to the organist's seat, we two plied all our united zeal in preparation and in carrying out this blessed work of love. Week after week meeting in the hall to practice music, and fitting ourselves as we should for the responsible place. Prejudice gradually gave way as they saw we meant to go through. In a short time we had many young friends on our list, and the school was pronounced a success. As for us, we rejoiced ; and whether it rained or snowed or shone we were always blessed with strength and purpose to be present. One snowstorm was so terrible that only the janitor and we were there ; but we went through the service all the same. One thing in my husband's character,—he had the "hold-on" feature, which characterized his work now in this blessed field as it did when, proprietor of the hotel, he persisted in making money behind the bar. This latter fact I never knew till after our marriage. A little incident right here I will relate to show how sweetly the Saviour shielded us from going back into old habits of intemperance. One day my husband brought home some baker's beer, which he said was "innocent." I looked at the white bottles for a moment, and then said firmly, "That may be, but I shall not taste one drop of it." He replied, "Very well, I shall not drink anything which my wife will not," and he forthwith took the beer back to the baker. When the day came for us to leave Camptonville, and we held the last session of Sunday school, many eyes wept, and we felt the power of the sweet, christian friendship formed therein, and also the keen sorrow of leaving those tender little ones to other hands.

The Revival.

Brother Hazen once appointed a time for conducting revival services. As we entertained him and the elder also we were all in readiness, and felt within us a strong desire for a holy life. We longed for something spiritual which was deeper and more satisfying, though at times the spirit melted us to tears at our family altar, and some friends who visited us were convicted also and blessed. We looked for a blessing which would be real and abiding. To this effect we attended the prayer meetings in the Welch church (there was no Methodist church in the place), just around the corner from us, until the brother who had charge closed the house. I remember yet the last night we went, not knowing but there would be a meeting. We sat a long time upon the steps, and then went reluctantly home. These and many others were the preparations for the promised revival, as we felt ourselves

Hungering and Thirsting After Righteousness.

The brother came at the time appointed, and put up at our house and opened the meeting at the Temperance Hall, where nearly all the religious services were held. The next day the pastor, Brother Hazen, while visiting some worldly people, was requested to attend a *May day picnic*, which invitation he accepted. When he stated to us his intention of stopping the meeting one day for that purpose we were incensed, feeling sure it would greatly interfere with the meetings in view. We plainly stated this to him, but he was incorrigible and would not be put off. As he was at 'our house we knew it would give occasion against us if we did not go ; hence

I baked a lovely cake, being determined in whatever I did not to be behind. We all went. The dear brother felt assured that "now we had them," and that in the evening they would all come and get saved. We all played the agreeable that day, and feasted upon good things and had a pleasant, worldly time. That night we all—the villagers—went, but *not to the meeting*. The greater part saved up the best part of the refreshments and had a dance party. Being disappointed, husband and I let these things hinder our getting the blessing. After all, the meetings were not in vain. Some good in answer to prayer was accomplished. One dear sister turned unto the Lord, others were revived, and we resolved to persevere in believing. Now we can look back and see that if we could only have believed for the blessing in the *present tense*, and not set a time in the future, and that depending on circumstances, we might have obtained it *then*.

> "Thus far the Lord hath led us on ;
> Thus far His power prolongs our days ;
> And every evening shall make known
> Some fresh memorial of His grace."

DEPARTURE FOR THE EAST.

For two reasons was the change made, namely, in behalf of my husband's two children in New York, at mother Peck's there, by request of their mother in her

last moments, and an interest in the property, previously
mentioned, which, in the mean time, had again been lost
to me in this way.   The party opposing me attached it
by charging me an enormous board bill as a last resort
of revenge.   I had been duly apprised of this by a sum-
mons to appear in a suit at law, which, after deliberation,
prayer and consultation with my husband, I concluded
not to do.   However, to offset this, rather to show the
unfairness of the proceeding, I sent in a bill for service
rendered during the time, which was greater than the
amount I was attached for.   I remembered the Scripture,
which says: "Ye go to law with unbelievers.   Why do ye
not rather suffer wrong?"   And I concluded it should
go by default rather than to appear.   It did.   We were
satisfied, and were willing to work and to trust.   It was
sold, and my previous lawyer bought it for a mere trifle,
as real estate had greatly depreciated in value.   Going
East, we stopped in the place to visit brother Willie and
his family.   Here some parties who knew of these mat-
ters came to us and informed us that there was a clause
in the law in the case in point where, if we chose to do
so, my husband could pay off the costs up to that time,
which were considerable, and hold the property in his
name.   We carefully considered it, and finally determined
that it would be right to do so, and especially in view of
the fact that at the first sale it had by strategy been
divided and offered in two separate lots, the one being
taken up by the child's mother and her husband.   We

supposed this would end the business without further litigation. My husband paid off all, and I made him a deed, and the rents, which had been accruing in the attorney's term of holding it, were now paid over to my husband. About or soon after this time we received word from Mother Peck that "she did not know how she could do without the children, as they were so much company for her in her recent widowhood." My husband said in reply that, "as she had cared for them when babes, now, as they were able to help her some, it should be as she said." Hence we located in the town of Reno, and this proved to be one of the best Providences yet experienced.

SEEKING JESUS

amidst such scenes of holding on to the things of the world, in a wavering way, is slow work indeed ; but as we were both really in earnest, desiring Christ, His mercy was very great to us. "Behold, how great is the goodness which the Lord hath lain up for those who love Him,—for those who trust in Him before the sons of men." In a manner I had done this from my earliest days. This fact, with all my double-mindedness, often manifested itself, and even in my earlier stages of grace sometimes made me the subject of ridicule. Take some incidents in question, though it be a disgression. While taking a course at a normal institute I was appointed

to select a piece from the reader and read on the platform at a stated time. I practiced a very pretty little
prayer, and reverently offered it up, looking heavenward,
as the case demanded, to the extreme amusement of some
pupils of very good taste in some things. Also, when
we as children, with our cousins and playmates, held
our prayer meetings, I would not allow anything other
than a solemn and reverent form of worship upon the
part of any of the younger children. I can hardly remember of hearing profanity, or anything rude or wicked,
without reproving it. Always seeking the exact right
in everything, yet not knowing how, by a present
faith for a present purpose, to always appropriate the
power of God, but seeking to exert my own power, not
realizing that my "righteousness was as filthy rags."
O, how wily is Satan toward one going on in an outward form of good works. However, the Lord suffers
us, and "we account His long suffering salvation."
However our cases may have appeared to others, we
were "preparing the way of the Lord" by adopting His
precepts, and seeking to follow them wholly. This
precious Friend we ever sought in His word, and in
daily prayer, "morning, noon and night." The regular
means of grace, the preaching, class meetings, Sunday school and prayer meetings, were regularly attended,
and taken part in with no small interest. Denouncing
sin wherever seen, and seeing it in others oftener than
in ourselves of course. The Saviour lets us out in that

way.   We can stand it better ; and at last in His mercy
He gives us an inner view *of ourselves*, and a willingness
to denounce and crucify *self.*

Two Incidents

will show our firmness in resisting some evils upon which
God was letting down light.   The silver wedding of
our pastor and wife in the church was made known by
expensive cards sent out by mail.   We, my husband and
I, even dared to get the ill will of those interested in this
worldly movement by declining the invitation in the
favor of some charity on the same night.   Another time,
when a festival was held in the church on a Saturday
night, and my husband, who acted at the time as janitor,
cleaned up for several hours the next morning, picking
the popcorn out of the thick woolen carpet, and upon
coming home found that he would not have time to dress
and attend church, deliberately declined that work any
longer, plainly and forcibly stating his reasons.   This
aroused a good deal of feeling on the part of some who
were in power.   As previously stated, our residence in
Reno was leading us to the very best of Providences.
We slowly yielded, yet *we were yielding* to His blessed
will.   After joining the lodge (I. O. G. T.) again in a
fit of temperance enthusiasm in Reno, the very same
difficulties arose as those which characterized the work
in Camptonville—lightness, lack of thoroughness and

aggressiveness. Again we retired from it. This time I
led out, and, while dear husband continued awhile longer,
I spent the long evenings in my room at our boarding-
house alone. Thank God! It drove me to Him with
more intense longing than ever before, as I clearly saw
that I could look to no earthly good for permanent happiness. The Lord was drawing us and "fashioning our
hearts alike," and soon my husband withdrew, after
making some stirring speeches in favor of a more aggressive warfare than the dry forms of the regalia and the
initiation and light society trifling.

HOLINESS.

There came at this time, after we had lived one year in
the town of Reno, a family from Oakland who took up
their residence in Reno. The lady, Sister Augustine,
came to the meetings, and husband and I recognized at
once in her testimonies and in her looks a victory and a
triumph of faith which we were not used to seeing, and
which we did not possess. We called upon her. She
professed the blessing of holiness of heart. She also in-
structed us on the subject, and our privilege and duty
of, at once, "entering in" by faith. This was Saturday
night. On leaving her house she placed in my hands
Hannah Whithall Smith's little book, "The Christian's
Secret of a Happy Life." I took it with me, and by the
next day had read enough in it to get much light as to

the way, the simple way, of claiming the blessing "*now*" by faith. These were all the Lord's helps, and not man's after all. And so sweetly He was leading when He saw our readiness, and *the yielding up of our wills*. After church the next day husband came to me and said, "I am not satisfied with my Christian experience." Said I in answer: "Neither am I satisfied with mine. Let us go at once to God and get the blessing of holiness." We went, and the blessing came. Jesus came. We approached Him in this way. First we knelt and sang a faith hymn,—the following :

COME BELIEVING.

"Once again the gospel message
  From the Saviour you have heard.
Will you heed the invitation?
  Will you turn and seek the Lord?
      Chorus.
Come believing, come believing ;
  Come to Jesus, look and live !
Come believing, Come believing ;
  Come to Jesus, look and live !

Many summers you have wasted ;
  Ripened harvests you have seen ;
Winter snows by spring have melted ;
  Yet you linger in your sin.

Jesus for your choice is waiting ;
  Tarry not, at once decide ;
While His spirit now is striving,
  Build and seek the Saviour's side.

Cease of fitness to be thinking ;
Do not longer try to feel;
It is *trusting* and not feeling
That will give the Spirit's seal.

Let your will to God be given;
Trust in Christ's atoning blood.
Look to Jesus, now in heaven ;
Rest on His unchanging word."

After singing these precious words and reading the
first chapter of Philippians, we, each in turn, poured out
our souls to God in earnest prayer.   The *witness of faith
was given me,* and I do not think I would ever again have
asked for the blessing so sure was I of receiving.   I
remember of believing that *the word* in this chapter *was
ours from God* to us *then* and *there for us in the blessed
fulfillment,* and that was *rest*—the *rest which faith brings.*
Hallelujah!   We arose sweetly refreshed, and, for the
present, satisfied.   The apostle in this chapter, by the
Spirit, had promised "peace" and "grace."   Thanks
were given for our "fellowship" from the first day until
now.   "*Being confident* of this very thing, that He who
hath begun a good work in you will perform it until the
day of Jesus Christ."   The apostle assured us that we
were "partakers of His grace," and "that He longed
after us;" and he prayed "that our love might abound
yet more and more in knowledge and in all judgment;"
that we "might approve things that are excellent;"
that we "might be sincere and without offense till the

day of Christ, being filled with the fruits of righteousness
which are by Jesus Christ, unto the glory and praise of
God." Upon these good things we stepped by faith and
soon felt the rock beneath our feet. Just analyze these
good words and look at them one by one :

1.—Gift of: " Grace " and " peace."

2.—" Thanksgiving for us."

3.—" Faith in His work in us."

4.—" Assurance that *we are* (*now*) partakers of His
grace."

5.—" Longing after us." (Think of it! even *longing
after us.*)

6.—" That our love might abound more and more in
knowledge and in all judgment."

7.—" That we might approve things which are
excellent."

8.—" That we might be sincere and without offense till
the day of Christ."

9.—" Being filled with the fruits of righteousness
which are by Jesus Christ."

10.—" To the glory and praise of God."

Could anything be more replete, more solid, more secure,
more satisfactory, more full of hope and comfort? I remember what a sweet and restful and quiet state of feeling
possessed us. At the time we said nothing more, as if
a real contract had been closed in with, and we had no
further apprehension as to the results. As for myself, I

remember of continuing my faith in this way—by occasionally repeating the words of St. Paul: " I am crucified with Christ, nevertheless I live ; yet, not I, but Christ liveth in me."

REVELATIONS OF THE SPIRIT.

The next morning, having adjusted all my work, my boarder and my husband being away from the house, and I alone, just after making my toilet, and while in the act of passing through the parlor, a glorious guest presented himself to me. He was Jesus, our Saviour. Quicker than I can write one word the light which filled and surrounded me revealed thousands of marvelous, wonderful and precious truths in Christ Jesus. His matchless beauty and grace shone down upon me, as He seemed to be standing at my right hand. In an instant His word with mighty power flowed through my heart, and witnessed to me the pardon of all my many sins. The peace and joy of this knowledge cannot be told. O, His love ! I stood in adoring silence,—in speechless adoration. In a moment I saw and knew that the Bible, from the beginning of Genesis to the end of Revelations, was *truth*, God's mighty truth. While these revelations were all within there seemed to come, also, a clearness of external vision ; the very grass on the lawn seemed to shine. A heavenly beauty indwelt and enshrouded me. He lifted upon me "the light of His

countenance." O, the love Divine ! it seemed to break
my very heart with its sweet and tender meltings. A
measure of all the graces of the Spirit was bequeathed
me, and, as far as *feeling went*, I was as pure as an
angel. Our dear Jesus stayed at my side, manifesting to
my soul's consciousness His glorious presence, giving
"*life*" for the first time. It was then I knew the meaning of that vital word, " Eternal life,"—" power"—for
the first time. I realized what the strength of Jehovah
meant. " Wisdom,"—my finite mind seemed for once to
know "wisdom,"—even Jesus, "who is made unto us
wisdom." "Beauty and grace !" Did I ever dream
that He, "the fairest among ten thousand," could be
half so lovely and gracious ? Indeed, I did not. Meek-
ness ! He, the mighty, grand and blessed God, seemed
to meet me,—to come right down on a level with me.
This knowledge seemed too great for me,—the weight
of it and the intensity of joy in my newly found treasure. The wonder is that I retained my consciousness
through all the heavenly ceremonies of this royal intro-
duction. Selah ! the psalmist was wont to write. He
failed to express the full meaning and delight of the
holy union. Would that I could tell the hallowed,
heavenly, tranquil serenity which pervaded my entire
being during this scene of my Saviour standing there
at my side in that humble cottage. I saw nothing with
the outer eye ; but feeling was now added to faith. I
knew Him whom my soul loved.

And thus it was, dear reader, that I became "a new creature," as "old things passed away" under the power of the Holy Spirit's revealings of my loving, living, risen Saviour. I do not remember of speaking to any one but once for three days. "I pondered these things in my heart." All this time the glorious guest was ever with me. I had come to "the waters of Shiloh, which flow softly," and I walked "softly," as if afraid my gentle, tender, precious One would withdraw His shining presence.

Now this was the beginning of what *I believed for*. This was incipient sanctification, the "new birth," the "living in the spirit," "forgiveness of sins," "justification by faith." Cleared indeed was I of all my committed sins; and *I knew it*, hallelujah! with a sense of continual joy. Sprinkled from an evil conscience, blessed regeneration, blessed quickening, blessed Saviour! Abba, Father, O, how dearly wert Thou revealed unto me in Jesus! Blessed Father, blessed Sanctifier! Glory to God. Thrice glory to God and the Father forevermore, amen! My feeling was that of *rest concerning my salvation*, and perfect satisfaction concerning everything. It seemed that my spirit was caught up into heaven, and the beatitudes of the eternal realm possessed me, filled me. Glory to God!

THE HOLY GHOST TEACHING ME.

Previously, I remember of thinking that such a sweet blessing as this would be the end—a kind of finish to the Christian life. But, behold ! it was only the *beginning*. I was now a babe,—a child of the kingdom. The Holy Spirit now in His tender love began to feed me, to protect me, to provide for and to teach and to guide me. I seemed enfolded in the arms of Almighty Love,—resting and getting strength after this transition from darkness to light,—just as the new born babe in its mother's arms lies softly, quietly sleeping, and drawing nourishment from her loving breast ; not realizing or knowing how, or thinking anything about it. Too safe and contented to speculate on these relations, and altogether unable to discuss them. But later on, as the little child is taught to beware of danger by running into danger, so was I of the spirit taught. At the end of the third day, it being May 30, 1883, my husband and I went to the opera house, where decoration services were being held. In taking this step I was all the while moved not to go. I really did not desire anything of the kind. Yet I went—my happiness all the while flowing on within. While there my face was so radiant with Heavenly joy as to attract the attention of even little children, and I longed to put my arms around them all, as my love flowed so abundantly.

The First Lesson.

As I before stated I really felt led not to go ; but once there I began, by my inward monitor, to know that even

with the show of goodness in such services it was no
place for me ; that I belonged to a kingdom not of this
world.   As the band poured out their loud strains of
national melodies ; and a certain lady, in all the possible
beauty of worldly attire, stood upon the stage reciting a
national poem. I knew that such honors were not in glory
to His dear name—whose I now was.   I resolved that I
would henceforth absent myself from all such worldly
associations in the future.   The services over, on our
way home my husband stepped into his store, and I
walked on alone.   Passing a millinery store, and hap-
pening to look at the show window, I thought of a wreath
which I had sometime previously made up my mind to
purchase, and 'impulsively started into the store.   In an
instant the Spirit impressed me not to buy the flowers.
As for me I felt instantly an aversion to anything of the
kind.   Having so precious a Saviour satisfied me, and I
knew that I did not now love wordly adornments.   But
my heart was so light and gay, and the saleslady seemed
so sweet, that just to please her I bought a wreath of
flowers for seventy-five cents, getting the cheapest one
possible.   But, alas ! as I passed the threshold of that
door Jesus passed the threshold of my heart ; and, instead
of " Christ within," that little straw-colored wreath was
hung up within for my soul to look upon.   O, what indescribable sorrow passed through me ; and Jesus, my one
loved treasure, had fled from my view, and an object of
loathing hung up in my spiritual sky insinuating itself

to my utter grief. I thought I should die to have Him thus absent Himself. My misery was utterly indescribable. I walked home and out into the yard, and as by the force of habit went about my evening duties, more mechanically than interestedly. And now the Devil set in with his temptations trying to cheat me with his voice, which I would not follow; for the Holy Spirit held His child still, though "for a small moment He hid His face from me." I trusted. My faith held as an anchor. Having seen and known my Saviour, how could I but trust Him. I felt that my feet were on the everlasting rock, and thus I was taught to grow up into Him, denying worldly pleasures. My faith was once more rewarded. As I walked into the parlor where Jesus first met me, and reflected upon these wonderful dealings, and sitting down upon a sofa,—behold! my dear Jesus once more appeared to me as before in all His loving nature and beauty; and then it was that I wanted to fall at His blessed feet, and to ask nothing more henceforth and forever but to lie there prostrate before Him, and worship His blessed name through all the eternal ages to come. But something besides enjoyment must come to the spiritual as well as to the natural child. There must be teaching; there must be work. In spite of this renewed presence to me, the matter of the wreath of flowers was not yet adjusted, and the next day it still clung to my mind, until this thought came to me: "I know what I can do. I can take my scissors and clip it off of the hat." I did so, and quick as thought it left my mind and never troubled me again. It paid so well—the sweet relief—that I went a step farther and cut off a long crimson plume from another hat. Thus one lesson was dearly learned, and wisdom gained therefrom concerning the vanity of worldly attire, and that our adorning should be "the hidden man of the heart, in that which is not corruptible ; even the ornament of a meek and quiet spirit, which is in the sight of God of great price" (1 Peter, iii : 4).

The Second Blessing.

Notwithstanding these marvelous workings more was to follow quickly. Hallelujah ! The fourth night of this walk in the Spirit I lay down upon a sofa, and, as far as feeling went, was perfectly incompetent to go to prayer meeting, as I was wont to do ; but, with my new guest to draw strength from moment by moment, I resolved to go— and go I did. My husband and I went together, as usual. Praise God for this beloved companionship. There, in that little meeting, I testified to pastor and brethren and sisters that my former Christian life had been a failure ; and that I had never known peace or pardon, or my precious Saviour, until the previous Monday morning. This was Thursday night. I then told them of my Sav- iour's manifesting Himself to me, and the blessed and gracious presence of the "peace which passeth under- standing." Feeling at the time that this blessing was entire sanctification, the Spirit's movings upon my heart seemed unaccountable, for I was thrown into a state of deep conviction right then and there,—a painful longing for something more, I knew not what. All I could pray for was for " all the fullness of God." This I did repeatedly. Then after testifying in that meeting, as conviction deepened within me, I consecrated again fully in these words of the hymn :

> "Lord, I am Thine,entirely Thine,
> Purchased and saved by blood divine ;
> With full consent Thine I would be,
> And own Thy perfect right in me."

And so left all with Him. The next morning about the same time our Saviour appeared to me as at first, and in the same room, no one else being in the house, all at once *I was filled with the Spirit.* A holy sensation as of tiny wings moved in my breast with an indescribably precious experience, proving in blessed illustration the Scripture in Malachi iv: 2 : " But unto you that fear My name shall the Son of Righteousness arise, with healing in His wings."

BAPTISM OF THE HOLY GHOST.

Looking up to Heaven as if for an explanation of this new revelation there came a voice to me, accompanied by a shower of praise expressed in the words : " Glory to God ! Glory to God !! Glory to God ! ! ! " How oft I repeated these words I know not ; but many,

many times I said them over and over as I walked
through the rooms and clapped my hands, rejoicing with
"unspeakable joy." I realized that this was what our
Saviour meant when He said to the woman at the well :
"But the hour cometh, and now is when the true wor-
shipers shall worship the Father in spirit and in truth,
for the Father seeketh such to worship Him. God is a
spirit, and they that worship Him must worship Him in
spirit and in truth" (John iv : 23, 24). My joy was
full. Like the blessing of pardon, this blessing of heart
purity was instantaneous, and it proved the *death-blow to
self.* Having received a new nature old things passed
away. The Divine Guest came in and spake to me in
thunder tones and with the quickness of electricity :
"I in thee and thou in Me ; " "Ask what ye will in My
name and ye shall have it ; " "Faith without works is
dead." This was in the voice of God and was heard
within. "They shall hear My voice," saith Jesus.
Would that I could describe the sweetness of that voice,
and the Heavenly effect as it fell upon the ear of my
soul. The Spirit fed me with many blessed words,
among which were these in Heb. xii : "See that ye
refuse not Him that speaketh, for if they escaped not
who refused Him that spake on earth, much more shall
not we escape if we turn away from Him that speaketh
from Heaven: Whose voice then shook the earth; but now
He hath promised, saying, Yet once more I shake not
the earth only, but also Heaven. And this word, Yet

once more, signifieth the removing of those things that are shaken, as of things that are made, that those things which cannot be shaken may remain. Wherefore, we receiving a kingdom which cannot be moved, let us have grace, whereby we may serve God acceptably with reverence and Godly fear; for our God is a consuming fire." These words made me tremble. You know, dear Bible student, God speaks of those who " tremble at his words," and He saith also : " Work out your salvation with fear and trembling, for *it is God that worketh in you* to *will* and to *do*, of his good pleasure." As I retired to rest under the influence of the Spirit's blessed teaching, a terrible trembling passed all through me, and I even laid my hands on my body to see if it were trembling ; but the shaking was within my heart,—in the old ruined *paradise* ; *that evil was moving out as God took complete possession*; and blessed be His name, He gave me *a view of my carnal mind*, and the sight would have been appalling but for His all-comforting presence. The death was painful indeed ; but the grand new life sustained by His power rose up in a living " tree of righteousness, the planting of the Lord." And the foul mass of corruption which lay dead could not contaminate or defile it; but instead it was nourished and beautified with the water of the *Euphrates* river, which flowed once more in streams of *"perfect love"* through its channels from the "hills of God," and I drank freely of its delicious fountain and was satisfied. This, too, was a conscious fact.

THE FIRE.

This came too, at first as a *pure* and *healing* burning, which I felt throughout my entire being *in a conscious way*. All these realities came in a much shorter time than it were possible to write them. And this, the baptism of fire, proved to be a very fitting prelude to the "fiery" ordeal of spiritual suffering in my union with the sufferings of our Saviour.

GETHSEMANE.

During these operations of "the Spirit that I might benefit withal," once in the midnight hour I was led by the Spirit out of my room into an adjoining one unoccupied, and there in a most mysterious way I was prostrated upon my face, and drank in with our dear Jesus of the agonies of the dark hour of His passion. There I tasted of His sufferings for a lost world. But, wondrous truth, this weight of unutterable pain was so lightened by His conscious presence as to make it throughout the very dearest of all the blessings yet experienced,— the blessing of sharing His sufferings. O, the blessedness of that midnight hour! How long I lay there on the carpet in the cold room with only my night-robe over me I cannot tell. But this, be it said most reverently, was only another of the precious love-lessons of our dear Jesus. And I rejoiced with "exceeding joy" that one so unworthy should be counted worthy to receive

such honor. "He that honoreth me I will honor,"
saith the Lord. It was this part of my experience
which proved the motive power to my soul-saving zeal.
I saw the awful scene of a world sinking into hell, and
the Saviour's loving arms outstretched to save. O, He
made it so real to my very heart. Glory to God !

A "WORD" LESSON.

On Sunday morning, after the baptism with its scenes
of death to self and life in Christ, I was led by the
Spirit to an east window in my room. *Realizing* "the
fullness of God," and lifting up my hands inclosing my
Bible, prayed for His word to be given me, and quick
as thought opened on the 121st Psalm. It seemed that
the Spirit did it, guiding my hands. With what sweet
spiritual joy I read this comforting word and promise. I
give it below; read it, please :

PSALM CXXI.

" I will lift up mine eyes unto the hills, from whence cometh
my help.

" 2. My help cometh from the Lord, which made heaven and
earth.

" 3. He will not suffer thy foot to be moved: He that keepeth
thee will not slumber.

"4. Behold, He that keepeth Israel shall neither slumber nor
sleep.

" 5. The Lord is thy keeper: the Lord is thy shade upon thy
right hand.

"6. The sun shall not smite thee by day, nor the moon by night.

"7. The Lord shall preserve thee from all evil: He shall preserve thy soul.

"8. The Lord shall preserve thy going out and thy coming in from this time forth, and even forevermore."

How precious this living water of the Word tasted to my thirsty soul. I drank it in and besought the Lord for more, when quick as thought the Spirit gave me

ISAIAH LIV.

"Sing, O barren, thou that didst not bear: break forth into singing, and cry aloud, thou that didst not travail with child: for more are the children of the desolate than the children of the married wife, saith the Lord.

" 2. Enlarge the place of thy tent, and let them stretch forth the curtains of thine habitations ; spare not, lengthen thy cords, and strengthen thy stakes :

" 3. For thou shalt break forth on the right hand and on the left, and thy seed shall inherit the Gentiles and make the desolate cities to be inhabited.

" 4. Fear not ; for thou shalt not be ashamed ; neither be thou confounded ; for thou shalt not be put to shame ; for thou shalt forget the shame of thy youth, and shalt not remember the reproach of thy widowhood any more.

" 5. For thy Maker is thine husband ; the Lord of Hosts is His name ; and thy Redeemer the Holy One of Israel ; the God of the whole earth shall He be called.

" 6. For the Lord hath called thee as a woman forsaken and grieved in spirit, and a wife of youth, when thou wast refused, saith thy God.

" 7. For a small moment have I forsaken thee ; but with great mercies will I gather thee.

" 8. In a little wrath I hid my face from thee for a moment ; but with everlasting kindness will I have mercy on thee, saith the Lord thy Redeemer.

" 9. For this is as the waters of Noah unto me : for as I have sworn that the waters of Noah should no more go over the earth, so have I sworn that I would not be wroth with thee, nor rebuke thee.

" 10. For the mountains shall depart, and the hills be removed ; but my kindness shall not depart from thee, neither shall the covenant of my peace be removed, saith the Lord that hath mercy on thee.

" 11. O thou afflicted, tossed with tempest, and not comforted, behold, I will lay thy stones with fair colors, and lay thy foundations with sapphires.

" 12. And I will make thy windows of agates, and thy gates of carbuncles, and all thy borders of pleasant stones.

" 13. And all thy children shall be taught of the Lord ; and great shall be the peace of thy children.

" 14. In righteousness shalt thou be established : thou shalt be far from oppression ; for thou shalt not fear : and from terror ; for it shall not come near thee.

" 15. Behold, they shall surely gather together, but not by me : whosoever shall gather together against thee shall fall for thy sake.

" 16. Behold, I have created the smith that bloweth the coals in the fire, and that bringeth forth an instrument for his work ; and I have created the waster to destroy.

" 17. No weapon that is formed against thee shall prosper ; and every tongue that shall rise against thee in judgment thou shalt condemn. This is the heritage of the servants of the Lord, and their righteousness is of me, saith the Lord."

The Fast.

To show the relation of this inward experience to that in the life of our Saviour, I would record a special experience just after receiving the baptism of the Holy Ghost, which lasted through the space of about forty days, and impressed me vividly at the time--the sweet and endearing nearness to Him in this inward life outwardly manifested. During all these days I cared not to eat. So deep was the fast brought on by this wondrous knowledge of Divine Life, I thought I should never care for bodily food. I ate a little occasionally, but after all it was one long fast. At the end of this period I was one day at the house of dear Sister Agustine, and all at once "I hungered." When I told her she prepared food for me with kindest attention.

Temptations.

These were strewn thickly all along. Very wily was the arch enemy, as he suggested to me to close my eyes while walking along some dangerous place in the street, and then when I would not he accused me of not trusting in Jesus, who was able to keep me even with my eyes closed. I felt as sure of that as he did, but I would not mind him. I might have said, "it is written," but I was a novice in divine things on that line, and the Father kept me and would not allow me to follow a stranger's voice. While sewing the tempter would sometimes say : "It is no use to go by patterns or measures ; just take the scissors and the Lord will guide your hand. The old enemy would impress me strongly with the comparative facility of such a course, and no one can imagine how I would suffer and be tried under this ordeal. But the Father looked on and strengthened His child by the Spirit's power. One day while at a friend's two dogs began fighting right at my feet, and in sudden alarm I ran from them, when Satan assaulted me afresh with, "You cannot be sanctified or you would not be afraid." Keen suffering always attended these moments for the instant, at least, on account of the sud- denness and emphasis with which his impressions were forced upon me. As time went on, of course, I learned to gather strength and victory right in the thickest of the fight. One day while in the act of taking a bath the enemy hurled this Scripture upon me, "Thou canst not make thee clean, though thou wash thee with niter and take thee much soap." His idea evidently was in some way to get me to doubt my inward cleansing.

This was the day after I was sanctified. I *knew I was clean*, but robing myself at once I knelt before God, and quicker than thought the Spirit made me know that it was Satan tempting me. I laughed outright for very joy at having such a blessed comforter and deliverer. I then resumed my bath with perfect rest. And thus was I taught the way of faith. I knew that I had been par- doned and sanctified by faith, and now I was being taught that I was to be "*kept by the power of God through faith.*" "He was tempted in all points like as we are, yet without sin." To tell of all the fierce conflicts on this line would be impossible. At one time I lay awake for a whole night resisting the Devil, who gave me intense suffering through temptation. I finally said aloud, "If I had to lay awake here and say it a thousand times, 'I will trust in Jesus,' I will continue to trust in Him." I then soon after got relief. At such times as these the Scripture, in 1 Pet. iv : 12, 13,—"Beloved, think it not strange concerning the fiery trial which is to try you as though some strange thing happened unto you : but rejoice inasmuch as ye are partakers of His sufferings, that when His glory shall be revealed ye may be glad also with exceeding joy,"—gave me sweet relief, and so I went on trusting. Hallelujah !

"Inasmuch as He hath suffered, being tempted, He knoweth how to deliver *the Godly* out of temptation." "God is faithful, who will not suffer you to be tempted above that ye are able ; but will with the temptation make a way of escape, that ye may be able to bear it" (1 Cor. x : 13). O, how often this precious promise has sustained and comforted my soul in the last ten years. Praise the Lord !

"Blessed is the man that *endureth* temptation, for when he is tried he shall receive the crown of life, which the Lord hath promised to them that Love Him" (James i : 12).

IMMANUEL.

To know Him is to love Him,
To see Him to adore ;
To walk with Him is bliss
And glory evermore.

Hold thou my hand, dear Saviour ;
My heart, O, seal it thine !
Thy spirit give to heal me ;
And all my powers refine.

I'm blest, I'm blest, dear Jesus ;
Just now Thou hearest prayer ;
A quiet calm pervadeth,
Removing every care.

Praise God, my soul most happy,
For sanctifying love ;
'Tis this sweet gift, O, Saviour !
Prepares for realms above,--

Where, in Thy glorious presence,
In heaven's fragrant air,
I'll praise Thy name forever,
With saints and angels fair.

PART II.

Work for Jesus.

AVING sought and found "the kingdom of God and His righteousness," "all things" began to be added. Among my first feelings was the consuming love and desire for the salvation of souls. Opportunity offered daily, and through my own bodily weakness the Lord worked mightily, "the spirit of glory and of God resting upon me." At an early *Sunday* morning meeting—the *first* after receiving "purity"—the Lord enabled me to testify to the baptism of the spirit and the precious result in the words of the hymn :

> "I have entered the valley of blessing so sweet,
> And Jesus abides with me here ;
> And the Spirit and blood make my cleansing complete,
> And His perfect love casteth out fear."

I most earnestly exhorted them to "believe and receive and confess Him, that *all* His salvation may see." O, the joy of that first Sabbath day in Canaan! I desired to take the whole world in my arms, as He poured His streams of love afresh through my soul. How I did praise the Lord with singing and with shouting. "He that maketh mention of the Lord let him not keep silence." As before it sometimes had been a cross to speak, so from this time on the order was reversed. The cross lay in keeping still. The whole church were stirred, the minister and class leader desiring that all might be thus blessed. But this was to be no—"Peace, peace, when there is no peace"—warfare, no "building with untempered mortar;" for the Holy Ghost was now at work. Blessed spirit of truth! The following prayer-meeting evening the spirit in me warned them to do as did the woman who lighted the candle and searched for the piece of lost silver. It was made so clear to me that the lost piece was heart purity. How I longed for the pastor to have all stay until by faith it was restored to each. Can you imagine how surprised I was when some of them so little realized its worth—its priceless worth—as to go off to the home of one of the members and hold a party that very evening? But God walked in me, and in a few days I found on my table a number of slips of paper, each bearing on its fair bosom a text of God's living truth. I was wondering how to use them, when in came two sisters of the church, and invited me to a surprise party for an old but fashionable lady in the church. God had a work there that night ; and little did that crowd realize the holy joy which filled one simple heart as I passed from one to another through that throng of professing Christians and handed a little slip of paper to each one of them : "How can you believe, which receive honor one of another, and receive not the honor which cometh from God alone ?" This pointed passage found its way among the rest, and cut deep into the convictions of many. In this ministry, however, the angry countenance of "the man of sin" was discernible on some faces. It was the same which at one time tried to cast Jesus of Nazareth down from the brow of the hill, just because He hinted to them, in the gentlest manner possible, that there were not many who "believed." In less than a week the pastor gave out that I was crazy. Now the "fight of faith" began in earnest, and it was the faith which was moved by *love.* "God is love."

STREET WORK.

Neglecting the rules of modern etiquette, these little white-winged messengers were scattered through the streets as profusely as advertisements or show-bills. And why should they not be ? They were thrown into windows and pushed under doors, as the child of God felt the necessity of arresting the attention of the masses concerning their neglect of God's offers of free grace, and the necessity of at once seeking to "flee the wrath to come." In doing this we realized the blessedness of "sowing beside all waters."

VISITING SLUMS.

"Condescend to men of low estate" (Rom. xii : 16).

We felt a desire to go down to the very lowest strata and "rescue the perishing." We felt a deep sympathy for those who had not been favored with good advantages or opportunities for coming to Christ. We pitied those whom we feared had never heard the Gospel message, and to these we went among the very first. And we did not go in vain. Under the door of a brothel this little text was slipped, "Go in peace and sin no more." This was followed up by a call upon the same person. One of the inmates of the place wrung her hands, and with streaming eyes confessed the power divine. Another promised to cease the life of sin. Others were drawn to us as by some unseen magnet. Another, who at first reluctantly received us, was through our prayers and personal dealings melted to tears, insisting upon kissing us when we left the house, inviting us to come again. Singing and praying and reading the word to them,— thus it was we went these rounds with much joy, heavenly smiles, or sometimes, if refused an entrance, we wept, and then and there drank in the sweet, sweet blessing of "going forth with weeping, bearing precious

seed,'' believing that in due time we would return bearing our sheaves with us.

SALOONS VISITED.

The word of God was published here also. Drunkards were often turned away from the haunts of vice by
this means. A brother who had formerly been converted
in the Salvation Army, but wandered away from it,
was given a Gospel tract at one of these dives. It was
the means of reclaiming him ; and he testified this to one
of the brethren with joy, saying he thought I was a real
lassie of the Army.

On a Sunday morning once, when one of these dens
was well filled with men, some songs were sung and tracts
given out to each, and speedily one young man went out
and was followed by all the rest, leaving the keeper alone
and in a rage against us. Approaching one on a certain
Sunday afternoon, a crowd was seen gathering in front,
and it was soon discovered that two men were fighting.
As it was out of the question to enter or to distribute
them in the usual way, a package of them was thrown
high up in the air, and, raining down a shower over their
heads, their attention was arrested. The tracts were
picked up by one or another, and the crowd dispersed.
Prayer was always the motive power in all these ministrations so unusual. The lower and more sunken in
degredation these men were the more they seemed to

appreciate these calls,—sometimes touching their hats
and bowing with unfeigned respect. We thought they
took courage, and a hope for deliverance from the chains
which bound them to the curse of intemperance. We
noticed a difference in the more aristocratic saloons, as
if they trusted in their respectability and more favorable
quarters and appointments, or perhaps in "high license."

Visiting from House to House.

So anxious were we to get the facts of God's blessed
salvation from a real experimental standpoint upon the
minds of the people, that I went oftimes alone "from
house to house telling the joyful news." Each day as
soon as home duties were done I made these rounds with
the Holy Spirit's attendance.

In many a humble home Jesus was accepted, oftimes
with tears and true sorrow for sin. Truly there was a
flocking home to the fold. "The poor shall hear thereof
and be glad." This scripture we saw fulfilled. On several occasions, as we stood at the door of some aristocrat,
and prayed this prayer, "Lord, let thy peace come unto
this house," some lady would come and bid us "depart."
We did, with much love, praying, "Father, forgive
them." Our peace "returned unto us." Recently I
met *one* of these ladies who did so as much as eight
years ago. She was very kind, and pressed my hand
tenderly. Who knows but she may yet be saved ? "Your

labor is not in vain *in the Lord*" has always been a very comforting word to us in all our work for Jesus.

CHURCH SERVICES.

These were punctually attended in the power of the Holy Spirit, a constant stream of testimony pouring through our hearts from the throne in the "Holy of Holies," within where our dear Jesus sat reigning in triumph. The continued exhortations to all to seek a more vital experience—even holiness—moved one woman with anger, and she wrote me an anonymous letter. I read it, and then laid it out upon the bed before the Lord, and kneeling there by my bedside I prayed the Lord for Christ's sake to sanctify the author of it. Soon my prayer was answered by the sister asking my forgiveness, and her profession of the blessing of sanctification.

I could not withhold an invitation for any and all who would do so to meet at our home for earnest seeking for deeper things in God. Quite a number came at first, and a blessed revival spirit was springing up, but Satan hindered, and the numbers decreased. Five of us, however, continued steadfastly to meet every week for prayer to our almighty and omniscient God to let down His sanctifying power upon His people. This was kept up, and in a short time three new ones were blessedly sanctified. Glory to God! These souls added to us began an aggressive warfare on sin, giving praise to their redeemer. A number of others began seeking the Lord, coming to our home in the intervals to inquire about the blessed way of salvation *through faith* in the *atonement* of our Saviour, desiring purity of heart through the precious blood of Jesus.

CORRESPONDENCE.

In the mean time hundreds of letters were written under the power of the spirit to distant relatives, friends, acquaintances, and even to strangers, containing testimony to the blessedness of the experience of holiness. Great good was done in this manner, all being convinced of their need of salvation,—some seeking it and others professing the obtaining of it,—among them a strange lady in Eastern Nevada, who was enabled, with great joy, to take Jesus as her sanctifier and her healer, and has since given evidence of a holy life in active Christian work in all the region where she lives, and success in winning souls for the past nine years, and she the most weak physically. So much for power divine. Hallelujah !

PERSECUTION.

The most of this came from luke-warm professors who disliked a holy zeal. Sometimes it came also through worldly channels. One Monday morning a neighbor said to me concerning our meetings, "Don't you think you are carrying them too far?" I begged her to explain her meaning. She then showed me in the Saturday evening's *Reno Gazette* (March 19, 1887) a little notice which I had not seen, and which I now transcribe :

"Another victim of the Salvation Army. Laura Larson, for some time past a domestic in the house of J. Novacovich, on West Street, was taken into custody this afternoon, charged with insanity. She is another victim of the Salvation Army, having, it is said, attended and taken an active part in the meetings held of late by Mrs. Peck. The demented woman is at times violent, and says that she personifies God Almighty. She curses many she sees, and tells of the flighty things preached by the Salvationists. Judge Bigelow will arrive in Reno on Monday, when action can be taken on her probable commitment to the asylum."

Previous to this, all slanders had been permitted to float out without a word of self-defense ; but we deemed that this should be replied to, hence the following explanation, which was published in the *Gazette* the following Monday evening.

EXPLANATION.

"RENO, NEV., Mar. 21, 1887.

"*To the Editor of the Reno Gazette* : In the cause of truth, and with all due regard to the readers of the *Gazette*, I deem it my duty to make a statement concerning the Saturday's report in the case of Mrs. Laura Larson. This person never attended one of our meetings. However, I remember of inviting her, as I did also Mrs. Novacovich and other neighbors and acquaintances, as opportunity has offered. The woman was only once in my house, and then only for a few minutes, in company with a child who belongs to my Bible class. I should possibly add that the meetings referred to are not under the auspices of the Salvation Army, as stated, but are merely private and quiet gatherings of a few humble souls who desire to lead Christian lives, and lead others, also, so to do. May this testimony be kindly received is my earnest wish, with the best of feelings to all, as mistakes will and must often occur. Respectfully,

"MRS. MINNIE H. PECK."

REVIVAL IN THE PASTOR'S ABSENCE.

From the time the blessed Holy Ghost came the fire spread, catching upon the garments of this or of that one, and burning out the dross of sin. Soon after Conference our pastor, Brother De Lamatyr, went East to attend the wedding of his daughter. This gave a few shining "lights along the shore" to blaze forth resplendently. Jesus was held up, and his word of life held forth in such manner that a gracious revival broke forth—a holiness revival. Blessed be God! Here some of our first fruits of sanctification "shook like Lebanon." There was "traveling in birth," and the dear spirit brought forth precious holy souls. One was the janitor, a lame and otherwise weak brother, E. F. Kirk. This revival continued for six weeks, many of the more zealous members attending with blessed quickening power. A copy of a testimony by Brother Kirk is given below, taken from one of the holiness papers.

TESTIMONY.

"PIKE CITY, CAL., June 23, 1884.

"*Dear Brother:* I feel moved to testify that the blood of Jesus Christ has cleansed me from all sin. In September, 1879, I was converted while working alone in a little alfalfa field near Los Angeles, and at once united with the Congregational Church in that city. But a strange feeling as of something lacking continually haunted me. Four months afterward I removed to Plumas County, and six months after to Sierra County. Up to December of last year my experience was that of a justified Christian. At times my spiritual state would be all that I could desire; and again I would be mourning in darkness and wretchedness. I felt all the time that this was not the state of a true Christian. I was convinced, in my own mind, that *there must be—was—a higher spiritual state,* in which one was continually 'full of faith and the Holy Ghost.' I strove mightily and blindly to reach it. I 'groped for the wall like the blind, and stumbled at noonday as in the night.' While in this state the spirit led me to Reno, Nevada, where I boarded with Brother and Sister Stone, two aged Christians in the same religious state as myself.

"Here, at the prayer meetings of the Methodist Church, I heard testimony to entire sanctification. Night after night an intelligent, refined, sensitive woman in feeble health stood up, and, in spite of the averted faces and silent opposition of most of those present, boldly yet humbly claimed heart purity by the blood of her Saviour. Deeply moved, I talked the matter over with Brother and Sister Stone, and they gave me the "Holiness Manual," by

G. D. Watson. As I read it aloud the spirit came upon me, enabling me to read it with power. Light flashed into all our minds. We saw that this was what we had been longing for, and resolved to have it. At this time I was janitor of the church. On my way to it one Sunday evening I determined to claim my privilege at once. After performing my duties I retired to a corner and prayed to be sanctified for His love's sake, asking Him to help my unbelief, then, rising, concluded my petition with the words, 'I believe You sanctify me, and shall act in that belief, trusting to You for the witness of the spirit.' No burst of feeling followed.

"At meeting next evening I claimed holiness through the blood of Jesus, but it was not till the third morning after my consecration that I received the witness; then, as we three knelt at the family altar, the Holy Spirit fell upon us with power, as upon the disciples of old. Dear old Sister Stone shouted aloud in ecstasy, while Brother Stone and I were shaken like reeds; but Thomas-like I conceived the idea that I had only shared Sister Stone's blessing; so my dear, patient, loving, tender Saviour gave me a blessing that I could not contain all to myself the next morning. How happy we were! Happy? No! that doesn't express it: how *blessed* we were. Morning, noon and night our cottage resounded with songs of praise, and we were enabled to 'speak the word of God with boldness.' The Scriptures seemed written in letters of living fire, and Jesus reigned supreme in our hearts. Then came the 'fiery trial' and shook our faith to its foundations; but it fell not, for it was founded upon a rock. We clung to Christ with the grip of drowning men, and He carried us safely through. Glory and praise and love to Him forever! My Saviour, I love Thee! My Saviour, I bless Thee! I am thine, wholly thine, forever! After that we were daily blessed with manifestations of the spirit and power, and, though now separated, yet we feel that we are one in Jesus. We are 'crucified with Christ, nevertheless we live: yet not we, but Christ liveth in us.' The Holy Ghost helps us to realize that we 'live *by faith*,'—a faith that must be exercised daily, hourly, momentarily. God has placed us on His 'Rock of Ages,' and put a 'new song' in our mouths. Glory to God! Good will and peace to men! And 'the peace of God that passeth all understanding' is ours. Dear blood relations in Jesus, pray for us ; we do for you. May our Father's richest blessings be yours.

"Your saved and sanctified brother,

"E. F. KIRK."

AT WORK.

Our dear Brother Kirk was at once led of God into the work of gathering with Jesus. A sweet and successful soul-winner he became, bringing, it is believed by those who knew him best, hundreds of souls "from darkness to light." His work continued in various places in Nevada and California for the space of about eight years, when he was taken from labor to reward. His death was a glorious one, full of rejoicing and praise to God ; and his last words were, "The blood of Jesus Christ, God's son, cleanseth me from all sin,"—as he gave them to the nurse in reply to her question whether he had any word to send to his friends.

Sister Stone has also passed away through great tribulation. Dear Brother Stone remains with us still, and if his eyes should ever rest on this chapter we hope he will take fresh courage, "fight the good fight of faith," and receive the crown of the righteous.

DOWN AT THE CROSS.

BY F. M. PECK.

I'm down at the cross for my cleansing,
    And I would lie low at His feet,
Who wrought out the plan of salvation
    In Càlvary's rugged retreat.

I'm down at the cross for my cleansing,
    That all that's of self may be slain;—
That Jesus may in me and through me
    Forever and ever remain.

Then I shall be humble and lowly,
    Submissive I'll be to His will ;
And "clay in the hands of the potter,"
    He fashions with exquisite skill.

And now as I lay on the altar,
    A sacrifice whole and complete,
I shall soon be a vessel of honor,
    For the Master's use made meet.

And now, in seraphic emotion,
    His love is pervading my soul,
And I am out on the ocean ;
    His infinite love makes me whole.

A vessel that's stranded and broken,
    No self for a mast any more,
In Jesus I've found a sure life-boat
    To bear this frail bark evermore.

And down at the cross for my cleansing
    Let me stay till life's labor is o'er ;
And then I shall gain the fair haven
    And rest on eternity's shore.

ANOTHER HOLINESS REVIVAL.

By the time that these events were occurring, the holy flame was fanning into a blessed fire all around us ; and by the coming springtime there was such an ardent desire for the coming in-gathering that a quartet of the soldiers of Jesus Christ in San Francisco were sent for and provided for, and the Methodist Church was brought into use for the occasion. The band who came professed the blessed experience of holiness, and some of them had been preaching it for years. I speak of our dear brothers Newton and Lawson, and sisters Sophia and Fannie Lawson. The meetings had been well advertised. Much praying over the anticipation of them had been done by the little band of five, who met once a week at our home. The pastor, Brother John De Lamatyr, was pleased, and every one in hearing distance interested. But, the best of all, the Holy Ghost overshadowed the town of Reno. The first meeting was held in the street in the center of town. Hundreds pressed their way to the place where the Lord Jesus was exalted in song. Old backsliders trembled. Drunkards listened with hope. Deep was the conviction upon all classes. From this meeting all were invited to follow around to the church that evening. They came until the church overflowed. The faithful little band of four—one of whom, dear Sophia Lawson, is now with the Lord in heaven—took their stand at the altar, and requested all who wanted a revival to come forward and

extend to them the right hand of fellowship while they
sang the hymn :

> "Jesus, my Lord, to Thee I cry;
> Unless Thou help me, I must die.
> O, bring Thy full salvation nigh,
> And take me as I am."

A most tender and impressive scene ensued, as nearly
every one in the house passed up the aisle and gave them
a hearty, and in some cases, a tearful, welcome. The
spirit moved a great upheaval of desire in the hearts of
the members of the churches in the place. O, what
beauty was in that scene, drawing souls into *"one accord,"*
—the only fitting prelude to the "baptism of the Holy
Ghost." The preaching was plain, forcible truth, presented with much endearing love. The Bible readings,
mostly by dear Sister Sophia Lawson, were beautiful,
with brief and pointed comments. The singing was in
the power of the spirit, and all this blessed work on the
line of a full salvation. The audiences from time to time
were charmed with "the beauty of holiness," and never
more so than when listening to the bright and joyous
testimonies to this sweetest "grace." The altar was
crowded nearly every night with penitent seekers of the
Saviour. Souls were dealt with personally and honestly.
Nearly all the members of the various churches were at
the altar ; and scores testified to a faith for the blessing.
To do justice to this work in writing it up would be
difficult. It was a work of perfect love, and every one

felt its precious power, and none more so than the dear children, many of whom were brightly converted, testifying to the same with sparkling joy. A Baptist lady and an Episcopalian brother, each of whom had once professed and lost the blessing, came out and started afresh in God's service. Confessing their sins, God was faithful and just to forgive them their sins, and to cleanse them from all unrighteousness. And great was their peace and joy in testimony and in work for God. One preacher and all his family sought and professed faith for holiness. A poor, sad drunkard returned to God, and made a triumphant exit from the saloon to the superintendency of a Sabbath school. Some of the very hardest cases of both sexes came weeping their way to Calvary; and what is better still, many, many of them, to my personal knowledge, are clinging to the cross of Christ ; and the influence now being exerted by them will, no doubt, be a glorious record in eternity. If any who look upon this account have wandered from God, we beseech . them in His name to return,—to confess and pray and trust, and start afresh in an entire consecration to Christ. And may God bless such, and all others who are drawing near "with a true heart in the full assurance of faith."

THE WORK SPREADING.

All through Nevada this blessed Gospel, preached not in word only, but in the power of the Holy Ghost,

increased and grew daily, God adding to us daily such
as were being saved.   After some weeks of work in Reno,
the band, accompanied by some of the home workers,
went to Carson, the capital, and for some more weeks of
blessed service immense crowds gathered on the street
and in the Methodist Church to hear the clear, pure, holy
Gospel of sanctification.   As a result a band was organ-
ized to revive the precious doctrine of God and His
Christ.   Virginia City was also visited with like precious
results. . Crowds of miners and citizens came flocking to
the meetings night after night.   The altar was crowded,
and many took on more faith for a better life, while
others repented and turned toward God for the first time.
It was a melting sight to see them falling under the convicting spirit's power.   O, love divine, all love-excelling,
naught can compare with Thee !   "God is love."   O,
blessed, perfect love, what canst thou not do for poor
sinners?

"O, 'twas love, 'twas wondrous love,
    The love of God to me ;
It brought my Saviour from above
    To die on Calvary.

Love brings the glorious fullness in,
    And to His saints makes known
The blessed rest from inbred sin,
    Our dear Redeemer's throne."

CRIES FOR HELP

ran all along the line.   Dear Sister Chrysler, a lady in
Eastern Nevada, having by faith recently "entered in,"
wrote us to come and help spread the "glad news."
The unerring spirit led us just at the right time, and
precious results followed.   She and I both weak bodily
(each afflicted with deafness), rode for many a mile on
horseback or in her carriage, visiting neighbors, miners
and others, holding meetings and distributing holiness
and general salvation tracts, books and Bibles.   As thus
we bore the message of salvation, we did realize that all
work for Him was sweet.   One morning we started for
a fifty-mile drive over the steeps, reaching the summit of
Mount Jefferson, the highest point in Nevada.   This
was in September.   Before nightfall a gentle rain came
down, and it became very dark.   Neither of us was
used to the road.   We were heading for Belmont, a
little county-seat, situated in a basin-like mountain-top.
At one time in the darkness we ran up the side-hill and
nearly upset, when she sprang out and guided the horses
into the narrow track.   Soon we saw the lights in the
village, and our gladness flowed right on.   A member of
the House of Representatives had previously invited us
to occupy his cottage in the absence of his family.   We
accepted.   All was lovely ; and the springing fountain
playing in the yard seemed a fitting emblem of the water
of life springing up and sparkling joyfully through our

hearts. Hallelujah! Sweet was our rest that night.
The following, taken from one of the holiness papers, *The
Herald*, will give an idea of this work of the spirit
through two little ones:

MISSIONARIES IN NEVADA.

"CLOVERDALE, ESMERALDA CO., NEV., Oct. 12, 1888.

"*Dear Workers:* Praise the Lord with us to-day for what He is
doing here in Nevada. 'He that diligently seeketh good pro-
cureth favor' is being sweetly fulfilled unto us, and our souls
rejoice. On September 29th Sister Chrysler and I drove fifty miles
through the valley, and over Mount Jefferson, 13,000 feet above sea-
level, reaching Belmont after night, tired but happy in Him whom
we love. The next day being Sunday we rested until 2 P. M., and
then walked around to the Church of England, where some young
ladies had met for singing and Bible study. They received us
kindly, as if by the Lord's own appointment, and we were invited
to teach them. All were agreed to take a step of faith, asking the
Holy Spirit to be our teacher. Our prayer was heard. The nine-
teenth Psalm was opened up so brightly before each soul that at
the close *every one* came to Jesus, the way of faith being made
clear. So victorious had been the word that we were requested
by some of the chief citizens to speak in the church that night.
However, the change from the sunny valley to a cold rain and
hail-storm on the summit rendered a longer rest necessary, and
Monday night was appointed. It came with richest blessings of
soul and great weakness of body. But this was God's opportunity, for 'when I am weak then am I strong : for the spirit of
glory and of God resteth upon me.' The choir, having taken a
step toward Jesus, opened up the way for them to lead in the singing, some more also coming to their help. The text taken was,

"Come Unto Me,"

and was so blessed of the spirit that at the close most of the audience, who were principally Episcopalians, signaled *their desire to come,*—and to come *into* '*all the* fullness ' of Christ. (It has been six years since they have had a resident pastor.) Among others, four young men and six young ladies rose. We praised God aloud. O, what a sweet presence pervaded that meeting. One week from that time, on Sunday evening, we spoke to a large audience from the words : 'To be carnally minded is death ; but to be spiritually minded is life and peace." The best attention prevailed, as a holiness sermon was preached. All seemed blessed, and at the close, at the suggestion of some leading sisters, a collection was taken. Nearly all contributed to the mission cause. One dear young man, just converted, and a member of the choir, gave five dollars. Dear Sister Chrysler being called away, I was left alone with God in this ministration of love. O, how sweet were His consolations of grace. Praise the Lord ! For ten days meetings and Bible readings were held, and children's meetings, and nearly every family in Belmont was called upon. The Bible was read, prayers were offered, and all exhorted to 'flee the wrath to come.' Only one woman refused to receive us. Surely the Lord gave us Belmont. Now these have started out afresh. Dear saints, help them by your prayers. All through these parts salvation is stirring the people. After a talk, songs and prayers with a strange young man, he took his leave, looking serious and saying, 'I think I shall do better from this time on.' Another dear young man, by the way, seemed so glad to hear us testify of Jesus. He said his parents, in Pennsylvania, were Christians. He gladly accepted a holiness book. All day long we are so kindly treated. One dear sister brought me twenty miles on my way, and gave five dollars to help defray expenses. The cry everywhere is, 'I do not understand the Bible.' These dear people want spirit-baptized helpers to lead them to our Saviour. O, what a harvest, and how few the workers. Infidelity is stalking through the land. Some little ones seeking truth are almost overwhelmed. One most touching incident occurs to me. I was in the parlor writing, when a pale, sick boy of about fourteen years came in. As is my custom, I began telling him what Jesus had done for him, and asked him if he believed it. 'I live at Rock Cabin, forty miles from here, and have come to town for medicine. I live with a man who says there is no God ; and I says there is, and we have a time. I have a Bible, and read it. I went to Sunday school in Eureka, W. T. *My mother was a Christian.*' This, then, was the boy's story. My tears flowed at the recital. How like a lamb among wolves was he ! I advised him kindly, gave him some tracts and a pocket hymn-book, when he said he must be off on his journey. Christians, some one must rescue these lambs, or eternity will show an awful reckoning. I take a ride to-night of fifty miles by stage. Will reach Sodaville by 2 A. M., scattering the seed of the word all along the way. How sweetly are we blessed. Once more we ask,—*pray for Nevada.*   M. H. P."

FIFTY MILES BY STAGE AFTER NIGHT.

"Lo, I am with thee always."

These words were sweetly fulfilled to me in taking the journey. The stage having broken down, we—the driver and one other pássenger and I—were compelled to ride on a vehicle called a buckboard, all sitting on the same seat together. The horses sprang wildly in their traces, and fairly skimmed over the ground on that bright, cold, moonlight night. There was not a house on the way, the only residents being the coyotes of the desert. Our trip was most prosperous, and on reaching

Sodaville the proprietor of the little mining village gave me a cottage with lovely and commodious appointments. While he made a fire for me he asked who I was. "A missionary," was the reply. He seemed ruffled, and said that "he was tired of them; the priest had just been there." When he left me alone in my snug little quarters I began my prayer for him, and for all the villagers, and was at peace. My rest that night and the next morning in the streaming sunlight of my room was simply heavenly. Just as my toilet was made a rap came and the door was opened. Mr. B——, my visitor of the previous evening, and his wife entered. Great was their enthusiasm as they informed me that they would have a meeting that night in the school house, and that they would convey me to that place in their carriage.

Expecting the spirit's guidance, I was not as much surprised as I was rejoiced. The day moved on grandly, that old Scotch Presbyterian lady making the rounds of the saloons and admonishing the men to quit drinking and come to the meeting. The Catholic school-teacher also invited them in from the "highways and hedges." In the mean time I visited all the families, distributing tracts and praying. Some promised then and there to come to the Lord and henceforth follow Him. That night my cottage had finally been selected as the place for meeting, and it was full of anxious hearers. *Holiness* drew together Catholics, Methodists, Presbyterians, and

all who came, down to the feet of our one common Lord,
our Saviour.   The Holy Spirit led the meeting, moving
in our hearts, giving us "*one* mind."   It was a pleasant
sight when the season of prayer began to see an old
Catholic gentleman motion to his little grandchildren all
around him to kneel and worship.   The word was read,
Salvation songs, with piano accompaniments, were sung,
and all present promised to admit the Saviour into their
hearts.   Truly we had a blessed meeting, some testifying
and exhorting.   When starting away the next morning
to board the Nevada Central Railway, and asking what
our hotel bill was, " Nothing," came the reply from the
same man who received us so coldly.   Here was another
open indication of His providing care and glorious presence.   Similar providences awaited us all along this little
tour,—a kind of wedding journey with our "Maker, who
is our husband" (Isa. 1, 4).   Hallelujah !

BATTLE SONG.

" The Lord of Hosts mustereth the host of the battle."

Tune : "Tramp, Tramp, Tramp."

Shout aloud the praise of God,
  Who hath conquered death and sin ;
He, "the way, the truth, the life," is reigning now
In the hearts of all the brave,
  Who have let the Saviour in ;
And He stands and knocks at other hearts to-day.

CHORUS.

Come, come, come, O, precious Jesus !
   Enter in and cleanse my soul;
For my life to Thee I give
As a living sacrifice ;
   And I now believe that Thou dost make me whole.

O, what glory beams within,
   When His lovely light I see ;
And His words so "quick" are flowing through my soul ;
And the blessed Holy Ghost,
   With the "precious blood" so free,
Enters, cleansing every portion of my soul.

CHORUS.

Stay, stay, stay forever, Jesus ;
   Thou art mine, and I am Thine ;
May my life abundant be
With the fruit of love to Thee,
   And Thy light upon my pathway ever shine.

VISITING ALL DENOMINATIONS.

As we have, therefore, opportunity, let us do good unto all men, especially unto them who are of the household of faith (Gal. vi : 10).

This work was of Him who is no "respecter of persons," hence none were slighted. Like Jeremiah, who said, "I was weary with forbearing, and I could not stay," or Isaiah, who cried out, "Here am I, send me," so were we with the blessed freedom and "liberty" of the spirit. Every church in town, even to the Catholic, was visited.

Personal testimony to a real, vital life in Christ was made, and the word attended with power. As a result all were quickened into fresh effort after a better life. The attendance was increased. The blessed doctrine of entire sanctification was brought to the light of open discussion and inquiry and teaching, from a scriptural and experimental standpoint. There was an increase in all the various churches, many of whom dated their conviction to the little work of visitation in these ways recorded.

PUBLIC MORALS.

These blessed influences, and the bold advertisement of the Holy Scriptures in public places on the highways, all had a restraining power upon all classes, checking immorality as they convinced "of sin and righteousness and judgment."

An agent one day waited upon our veranda listening to a song of praise, and then entered, inquiring, "Is it you who puts up these Bible posters upon the bridges, houses and fences?" He then assured us of the good he knew them to be doing as he traveled through the country. O, how simple is the plain Gospel of our Lord Jesus, and the methods which the Holy Spirit adopts to bring men to repentence. He takes "a worm to thrash a mountain," and chooses the weakest instrumentalities often with which to accomplish His vast and blessed purposes of good. The blessedness of such work in His name is beyond description, and can only be experienced to be enjoyed. All work for him is sweet.

RENO AND ALL NEVADA,

being by this time pretty well worked by "gathering out the stones" and preparing "a way for the people," our hearts began to be drawn to fields in the distance for personal work. To this end the Lord led some of us to San Francisco and Oakland, where, as before, it was aimed to reach as many as possible on the way and in these cities, with fresh testimonials to the almightiness of God's blessed salvation. In great weakness, tracts were distributed, testimonials and exhortations given in many places where opportunity offered. Some little acts of self-denial on this journey led to a plain illustration of tho Lord's providing care. Money had been given to purchase a morning robe, but it was laid aside for God's poor in the city. Soon after reaching our destination, at the home of a sister, she said, "Minnie, I have a couple of wrappers for you, if you will accept them." If our dear Saviour had spoken we would not have been more certain of it being His direct providence. I accepted them thankfully. Either of them was of far more value than possibly could have been purchased with the money. They were not only comfortable, but lovely, and, what is stranger still, they fit me as though they had been cut from my measure. Such incidents as this were scattered all along this heavenly journey, as if to inspire our faith,—resting, trusting, working.

IN SAN FRANCISCO.

While at supper my dear brother Willie was pleaded with to close in with God in a full surrender and faith for His acceptance. A gentleman overhearing the conversation became convicted, and went that very night to the Adelphi Holiness Mission, and sought the Saviour and started for heaven, acknowledging as he did so that the pleadings of a "saved woman" induced him so to do. The dear brother, also, in time, seemed to take hold of God in faith, and it is hoped was saved and is now in heaven. Eternity alone can render to us the full result of these labors of love. But this is sure, when the Holy Spirit comes to abide in our hearts we henceforth take our journeys and perform our labors, not for our own pleasure or profit alone, but "that by all means some may be saved." 'Tis then we look back at the trials and labors and hardships endured in and for sin, and with a holy reliance on God, and a boldness and determination born of heaven, we say: "Yes, Lord, I'll do this for Thee; I'll suffer for Thee; I'll die, if need be, for Thy glorious cause, counting not my life dear unto myself, that I may finish my course with joy and receive the crown of righteousness lain up for those who love

Thee." For the space of six weeks in San Francisco and Oakland the true testimony and the blessed word of life was held forth in various places of Christian worship, adding our little stream of love to the vast ocean flowing on and on in that blessed high tide of holiness which at that time was sweeping over many, many hearts as God's sanctifying grace took hold upon them in saving power. Hallelujah !

COTTAGE MEETINGS IN RENO.

The tide of spirituality ran so high that often we were invited by the people to come to their houses and hold meetings. These invitations were always gladly accepted, and proved to be scenes of great blessedness, a goodly number making their first determination to follow God during these meetings. Sometimes every one present united with one accord to seek and find the Saviour.

THE JAIL IN RENO,

and jails and prisons in other cities also, were visited at stated times, and the inmates preached to orally or by means-of printed sermons when open meetings were refused us. Salvation literature was most plentifully sown ; Bibles were furnished. Most gladly the prisoners gathered at the grates to be ministered to in this way.

Hospital for the Poor.

This place for years was regularly visited on Sabbath days, and religious services held in the large wards. The result was that many poor, sick men and women were blessed from time to time, and hundreds professed their faith in God, and their determination to follow Him to the end of life's journey. Some went out when well, and others died there in the profession of salvation. One old brother, a member of the Methodist Church, was thus visited and encouraged in the faith for a number of years, and, upon the occasion of his funeral, his son, a policeman in Reno, begged us to ride with him and a young friend of his. On the way home from the cemetery he also was dealt with about his soul, a pocket Bible was given him, and a promise obtained from him to turn unto the Lord. These scenes were at the time very touching, as the spirit worked upon hearts and moved us forward in holy triumph. The sweetness of the work as enjoyed by us in those by-gone days is precious to think upon, as day by day the work rolled on. Every device was thought of to awaken people to the need of coming to our Saviour. Willing hands find ready work.

Tract Boxes

were put up at our front door and at our kitchen door, and were kept supplied with fresh, hot salvation and temperance tracts; and very few agents or tramps got away without a little love-feast in this rare form. Boxes were put up in the postoffice, depots, and in one church, where we were gladly given permission ; they were no doubt the means of good being accomplished. We are certain that *one* of these tracts at our front door led to the conversion of a husband and wife, they in turn taking up this precious work for Jesus.

DEFINITE MEETINGS FOR HOLINESS.

In the mean time there sprang up a work for the definite teaching of the doctrine of holiness in the form of Bible holiness readings. These meetings were in the central part of the city, and invitations extended to all interested to be with us. The arch enemy fought *this* more than any other *form* of our Christian work ; but He that was in us was greater than he that was in them, and many precious souls came to "the fountain opened for sin and uncleanness," and professed faith for heart purity. Being novices, and with a very imperfect outward organization, many defects existed in this work ; yet we are not sorry it was started, and would be glad to have just such a work without the defects going on steadily in every city, town, village and hamlet. A saloon-keeper's wife and some of her children were brought to Jesus in these meetings. One day a poor drunkard, looking most degraded, came into the meeting and begged us to pray for him, but requesting us not to tell any one, as he did not want his comrades to know it. We knelt and prayed together.   He soon was blessed and led a different life, professing even the blessing of sanctification.   However, he left Reno and for awhile seemed backslidden, but the Salvation Army, now at work in Reno, have enabled him to be reclaimed, and he is now a steady worker in the rank and file.   Hallelujah!   Many others gave up their tobacco, liquor and opium and consecrated to God. Flowers, feathers, ornaments and hurtful articles of clothing were given up by the women, many of them, and in their place was entire consecration to God, and "hungering and thirsting after righteousness," with the blessed experience in some cases of being filled with the spirit.   Glory to God!   A good majority of these, to our knowledge, are still "holding fast the profession of their faith," some, it is true, in humble places, and others in more prominent places of Christian work.   To God be all the glory.

CHILDREN'S MEETINGS IN RENO.

"Suffer the little children to come unto me, and forbid them not."   To show the simple starting of this work among the little ones, which ran through a number of years, and is now carried right on in another form, namely, meetings for "Young Soldiers" (in the Salvation Army), I will copy from a Christian paper, under date Reno, Nev:, November, 1886 :

"You will be glad to learn that the Lord is still with us, and leading gloriously.   Over a year ago, while out one Sunday distributing tracts on the streets, I saw four little girls who went to no Sunday school. I requested them to come into my room, and we would have a Bible lesson (I will just state that these little ones almost lived in the streets). They came in, and we looked into the first chapter of Genesis. The lesson over, when they were leaving, to my surprise they asked if they could come the next Sunday. I seemed at once to see the hand of the Lord, and of course said, 'Yes; I would be glad to have you.' The next Sunday they came and brought another little waif with them, and thus increasing from time to time, with steady work on that line, along with other precious gleanings for the Master, we have got the blessed word of free and full salvation to thirty-two children in all at the children's meetings, and the number is steadily increasing. Glory to God! These little ones have been taught practical and present salvation from all sin, and they are really accepting Jesus as their Saviour. Six of them, boys from ten to sixteen, were at our Wednesday night meeting, and testified to their faith in Jesus to save them from their sins. Now praise the Lord and pray for us. I am still in the blessed work, 'rejoicing evermore, praying without ceasing, and in everything. giving thanks.' You will be glad to hear this, I know, and what the Lord is doing in our souls. I can truly say that the way grows better and brighter. O, praise the Lord! The half cannot be told of this grand and glorious 'highway.' In tracing the journeys of God's chosen people of old, and even the countries of the Holy Land, we find all are interspersed with waters, hills and valleys. So it is with us in the fulfillment of those types. Blessings in the valleys, glories on the mountain tops, and. sweet, fresh supplies from the river which flows from God and the Lamb. Remember me to all who are in Christ Jesus. My prayers ascend daily for the blessing upon all, and for a glorious outpouring of the Holy Spirit upon the work of Holiness upon this Coast. We have never yet forgotten the hour of prayer at sunset. Pray for us and the work here.   Yours, kept in the Beloved,   M. H. P.''

9

THE CHILDREN.

At the very beginning of this work the little ones said to me, "We are inviting all the children who do not attend Sunday school to come with us." When they themselves were invited to attend Sunday school, they instinctively hesitated on account of their poor clothing. The Lord, by His spirit, led these dear little lambs, and provided them clothing, and supplied all their needs. One of them lacked a Bible. The Monday morning after, I just spoke to Jesus about it, and in a few minutes the Methodist pastor came to call, and when departing put a piece of silver into my hand, saying, " For the mission." I praised God, and before night little Emma Hanson was rejoicing over a new Bible. Truly, the steppings of the Spirit with us are wonderful. "No good thing will He withhold from them who walk uprightly." Some time after this occurrence, when passing through the town where this child lived, we wrote on that we would stop off over night, and this little one, with her sisters and trusting mother, made us welcome, and had already invited others in, supposing we would, as usual, have a season of worship, which we did, and found that the mother and children were still leading a life of prayer and praise to their Great Deliverer. Hallelujah! They entreated us to remain longer, which we did. A meeting was held. Jesus' name was exalted, and salvation flowed. " A little child shall lead them " was truly manifested here. He had kept his own little ones in the fear of God, and obedient unto his word. This was the family of a saloon-keeper, who himself, in answer to our prayers, had removed his business away from the home of those little ones.

> There is none too high or none too low
> For our Saviour's love to reach.
> O, blessed be God ! He bids all come,
> And salvation he gives to each.

THE WARFARE AGAINST SIN.

F. M. PECK.

The mighty hosts are gathering ;
  I see them near and far ;
In every land and nation
  There is salvation war.
The contest now is growing hot ;
  The Devil's army rage.
Against the light of God they fight,
  And all their powers engage.

Fierce seems the conflict—sinners doomed ;
  An awful hell they see
Awaits the lost—forever lost—
  Through all eternity.
O, who can stand 'gainst God's command !
  Defy His mighty power,—
Who says "repent" of all your sins,
  Be saved this very hour ?

To God I look with weeping eyes ;
  To Him I breathe this prayer :
O, save the lost at any cost,
  My Father, Thou canst spare.
The vilest sinner Thou canst save,
  Though crimson is the stain,
And make Him as the driven snow,
  Until no spots remain.

Fight on, ye messengers of God,
  Lift up your voices high ;
The watchword pass along the line,
  And raise the battle-cry :
"Salvation *now*, in Jesus' name."
  Stand in His strength alone,
Till it shall echo o'er the land,
  And pass from zone to zone.

This mighty warfare soon will pass ;
  The end is drawing nigh ;
And soon will come the day for us
  To lay our armor by.
'Twill either be a victor's crown,
  And with our harps in hand,
Or wailing with the lost in hell,
  Forever with the damned.

VISITING THE SICK

was a specialty of a certain number of the workers. We
visited them singly, or in companies of two or more, as
opportunity offered. To tell of all these cases now would
be utterly impossible ; but as we look back over the field,

and think of some special and hopeful work on this line, we cannot but feel that on that great day we shall hear the Lord say, "I was sick and ye visited me."

A little child lay sick with pneumonia. She belonged to our children's class. She had not spoken for some time, and her mother shook her head in alarm. We knelt by the little bed where she lay, with the fumes of tobacco smoke almost stifling, as her father, in spite of our remonstrances, kept smoking. We offered a few words of prayer, while our tears fell fast in sympathizing sorrow for the dear little one. Then we began singing, and as we came to the chorus the dear child took on strength and raised up in the bed, and with sweet but weak and tender voice began :

"Rejoice, His name is Jesus, for He saves;
Rejoice, His name is Jesus, for He saves,
For He saves, for He saves,
For He saves His people from their sins."

Be it said, to the glory of God, she was soon able to rise and attend the meetings.

Another case comes to mind of a child whose mother had expressed a desired to be saved. Sister Jolly and I visited her. The child was very sick, having hemorrhage of the bowels, and her face was flushed with fever. The mother gave herself up to God to be ever His. We all knelt around the child, and each of us poured out our souls in prayer. When we arose the child got up with a sprightly air and ran off to play with the other children.

The sister and I then left, and as we went out she asked if I had noticed the little one's face,—how the fever flush had changed for the natural color. Of course I had. She then told me that the mother had called her attention to it, believing that Jesus had healed her in answer to our request. We could not but think the Spirit had done it to inspire her new and struggling faith. Some time afterward the mother informed me that the child had been well from that day.

ANOTHER CASE.

One day my husband informed me that some girls in the slums came to his furniture store to have a bed supplied for a sick one who had recently come into the house, and who was in a dying condition, caused by blood poisoning from smoking cigarettes, and given up by the doctors. Two of us went that very day. We found her alone. Her lower lip was swollen to terrible proportions. We at once went to the rescue with a hearty faith. The precious Gospel of Jesus was read, urging her to accept it. Songs of praise and salvation were sung. Our petitions went up to the throne. The poor, erring girl repented. She took hold of God by faith, and with hopeful countenance promised to be His child. We left her rejoicing in hope of recovery. She was soon on her knees, and her attendant found her there, and the two began to weep over their sins, and then to sing praises to God for faith for forgiveness. They promised to be as true to Him as they had even been to Satan. The girl recovered.

One More Visited.

On hearing one evening of an accident of a man run over by a train, by which he came to a speedy death unprepared, we were much grieved to hear this news, followed up with the intelligence that his wife, who had heart disease, was also sick and dying, and, still worse, a wicked woman, *unsaved.* I was led of the spirit to go to her, though she was a stranger, having seen her but once, and that in the interval of her husband's death, and then strangely drawn out after her, offering a prayer for her as I passed by where she was standing in her father's store. Upon entering the room where friends and neighbors stood around weeping, I asked the father if I could sing. He replied by bowing his head. Soon I was by the bedside, singing:

> "O, love beyond our highest thought,
> That from His throne of glory brought
> The Son of God, His life to give,
> That sinners lost through Him might live.
>
> #### Chorus.
> He died for you, He died for me,
> He bore our sins upon the tree;
> He died for you, He died for me,
> O, praise the Lord! His grace is free.

He took on Him our mortal frame,
A man of grief for us became ;
· He laid His robe and crown aside,
For sinners lost he bled and died.

His precious blood that flows to-day
Has paid the debt we could not pay ;
Come, weary souls, for refuge hide
In Him who once for sinners died.

Whoever *will* this hour may prove
His pardoning grace and boundless love ;
' Whoever will ' His child may be,
And shout with us, Redemption free."

She seemed almost gone.　Her face and hands were pur-
ple, and the latter deathly cold.　As I leaned close to her
ear and sang low and gently, she opened her eyes, turned
toward me with a loving smile of gratitude, and thanked
me over and over again.　I then asked if she believed
these sweet promises of God, and repeated : "This is a
faithful saying, and worthy of all acceptation, that Christ
Jesus came into the world to save sinners."　She nodded
her assent with earnest emphasis and triumphant look of
faith ; and, also, when I continued : " For God so loved
the world that He gave His only begotten Son, that
whosoever believeth on Him should not perish, but have
everlasting life."　The faith was then given me to pray,
and ask God to save her and take her to heaven for His
glory.

That night I called again, and her spirit had just
taken its flight.　Those who were present told me that

she died crying mightily unto God. It was believed she was sweetly saved at the last moment. Glory to God !

These are a few of the many cases of sick ones visited where a hope of their salvation was by the Holy Spirit made clear unto us. "As your faith is so shall it be unto you," saith the Lord. "Every one that asketh receiveth." O, how precious the promises, how certain, how full of truth ! We may, if we will, change the verse of the hymn and triumphantly sing :

O, our faith it is so simple,
And we take Him at His word ;
And our lives they are all sunshine,
In the glory of the Lord."

HOSPITALITY.

The early habits of our childhood training linger with us in the ministry of the saints and in remembrance of the poor. This has been one of the chief ways in which my dear husband and I have sought to honor God since first we started to journey together, often in great bodily weakness ministering in this way of our strength and substance, and *always* with a blessed *renewal* of *strength* and *substance.* Bread is yet returning unto us. Truly His supplies are bounteous, without stint, inexhaustible. "There is that scattereth abroad and yet increaseth," has been sweetly verified unto us, and all these years of our walk in the Spirit "we have lacked no good thing," but a full return of the promise, "It shall be given to you good measure, pressed down, shaken together and running over." Marvelously, mysteriously and lovingly hath He led, defended, supplied and kept us. But we have, in the midst of these ministries recorded in this book, toiled daily, working with our hands, "that we might have to give to those who were in need." We are finding that "It is more blessed to give than to receive." As we minister unto others He ministers unto us, and the joy of obedience and a good reward is ours. When oftimes our feelings of lost strength were almost overwhelming, one look upward brought down a quickening of our mortal bodies by the Holy Spirit's overflow from our full hearts into the channels of our physical being.

In childhood we were wont to use the adage, "Get thy spindle and distaff ready, and God will send thee flax." So in the spiritual preparation within, when all is made ready for the Lord, He by the Holy Spirit's power supplies all our need "according to the riches of the glory of Christ Jesus our Lord." This fullness of God's gracious indwelling is simply grand. The thousands of avenues which the soul thus surrendered and replenished finds for service, pouring along the blessed channels streams of light and love and peace and joy. Hallelujah !

> "The half has never yet been told
> Of love so full and free ;
> The half has never yet been told :
> The blood it cleanseth me.

O, Saviour, blessed Saviour mine,
What will Thy presence be,
If such a life of joy can crown
Our walk on earth to Thee."

SEPARATION.

Blessed are ye when they separate you from their company
(Luke vi : 22.)

It required grace for this as well as other commands.
It seemed so unreasonable for other professors of the
religion of our Lord Jesus to withdraw themselves from
us and really separate us from them when we had such
a sweet "secret" to tell them. The ministry who had
only a scholastic or a theological education seemed our
especial foes, and they, themselves not "entering in,"
hindered those who were entering in. This we clearly
saw with great sorrow, but "His grace was sufficient,"
and the Lord worked in us mightily. There was a constant "fight of faith," and our warfare was with spiritual weapons, as the great need of work for God on the
line of purity of heart was shown us in all these provi-
dential dealings. Never did Satan shoot at us in this way
with his poisoned darts from false shepherds, but that the
truth was given us with power to overthrow it. To
relate the definite manner of these frequent battles would
be almost impossible, they seemed so varied and yet so
hostile. In all their blind leading our Jesus worked by
His Spirit for the good of his little ones, who trusted

in Him, and often when by faith, naked faith alone, we were so sure of present victory, when everything looked the reverse, we have had to cover our faces with our hands to hide the smiles of holy joy springing from inner wells,—as to have openly rejoiced under such outward indications of defeat would have confirmed their opinions of our aceticism. Holiness gives the charity which "beareth all things, believeth all things, hopeth all things, endureth all things, which suffereth long and is kind." Hallelujah !

> "'Tis so sweet to trust in Jesus,
>   Just to take him at his word ;
> Just to know, thus saith the promise,
>   Just to know, thus saith the Lord.
>
> Jesus, Jesus, how I trust Thee,
>   How I've proved Thee o'er and o'er ;
> Jesus, Jesus, precious Jesus,
>   O, for grace to trust Thee more."

SEEKING SALVATION FOR RELATIVES.

Herein lay the hardest battle. Our love for them so intense with holy zeal, our views of the danger of delay, Satan's constant and determined purpose to hinder us every step, and their own misunderstanding and misrepresentations of almost every look and act of ours for them. O, holy soul ! was there ever just such a hard and constant and sore conflict ? Only that of thine own, if, indeed, it could have been so great, which I doubt, awful as it truly was. In thus waiting, often through

weary years, our souls have cried "out of the depths,"
" *O, how long !*" And then we would rejoice and sing
aloud while waiting at His blessed feet and upon the
solid rock of His eternal truth. "Ask what ye will in
my name, and ye shall have it." "Faith without works
is dead." Some of our loved ones have passed away,
leaving words and works, which bid us hope that we
shall meet in heaven. The first was dear brother Willie,
followed speedily by my niece, Minnie Pearl, just blooming into a useful life ; and then the mother, dear sister
Effie, was the last to leave us, until the reunion beyond.
Others remain here on earth at this writing, still the
objects of our prayers, some of whom are testifying to
the power of God to save and of an active faith in His
sweet work. So we thank the riches of His precious blood,
which "speaks" and "washes us whiter than snow,"
and "rejoice evermore." Hallelujah ! Working for their
good, trusting not in the works, but realizing that our faith
for them is more restful and perfect if we thus obey.

Always seeing that the sweetest blessings of all kinds
lie along the line of obedience to His every command :
and thus the days go by ; and at evenfall a hallowed
feeling of tranquillity rests down in our souls, oftimes too
deep for utterance, and we leave our loved ones in His
dear hands and his sweet will. Amen !

> "Thy various messengers employ,
> Thy purposes of love fulfill ;
> And 'mid the wreck of human joy
> Let kneeling faith adore Thy will."

A Seven Months' Tour.

On April 4, 1889, with my dear husband's approval after much united prayer, we were led of God that I should make a journey to the Atlantic Coast, visiting friends, relatives, strangers and all classes possible for the glory of God, and on returning bring my husband's sons, with the express view of endeavoring to bring them to God, husband desiring and expecting to join us and return with us to the Pacific. My first day of travel over the Union Pacific Railway was grand in the success which the blessed Spirit gave me. Some brethren in San Francisco had sent me several thousand tracts, which, with as many more of my own, I deemed a good start for train work. Being consciously led of the dear Spirit my faith and hope mounted up even in the trying ordeal of parting with my dear companion and coworker in Christian labor. At the depot I began the work of distributing and testifying for Jesus. The day was bright, and every one seemed to be pleased with the thought of our dear Saviour as His name was once more held up before the people. The train I took was an excursion train, and full of tourists,—ten cars in all. Permission was given by the conductor to work in each one. As salvation tracts full of pointed and loving appeals and testimonies were given to each one, conviction moved upon their hearts. Some professed to believe ; others slighted the Spirit and went on with their cards and games. Some made sport in order to shake off the movings within, but God turned it all in favor of truth. It happened that I had not secured a berth before starting, and all the sections in every car were taken. Little did this move me. On my feet most of the time, but the delight of my soul was great, and I felt nothing but the sweet strength of Jesus. At night a little crowd of passengers were standing conversing with the conductor, when I joined them. The conductor turned to me and said ;

"Are you now happy in anticipation of standing up all night?"

"Yes," I replied ; "I would be happy if I had to sit out on the platform all night." I then asked : "Are you happy?"

"No," said he bluntly.

I kindly reminded him that it was because he was not saved,—"A saved person cannot help being happy from the very outflow of internal conditions."

Just then, while musing upon Satan's impoliteness,— so unnatural in a conductor,—a gentleman joined us, and remarked to me, "I learn that you have no berth for to-night," to which I replied that I had not. He then stated that his wife and he had a whole section, and that they had been using the bedding of the upper berth to make theirs more comfortable, but that if I would accept the upper berth they would gladly let me have it. His kind way in this Christian act of goodness, assuring me that he would desire to have his wife or daughter so

treated, caused the little company to see the providence
of God,—the care of His child.   As for me, my thanks
and gratitude were offered heartily, as I proposed to pay
him for the berth.   He would accept nothing.   Neither
would the porter accept anything for his service.   This
to me was the sweetest night I ever spent in a car,
although I had worked in trains before.   My glad
work all the day long gave me such a clean conscience,
as I ascended the stepladder to my little berth, and
there I knelt in cordial praise, praying His blessing
upon the conductor, engineer, the trainmen and all passengers.   O, how refreshed was I as I arose to begin
another day for Jesus.   No weariness, no headache, as
was always my former experience in traveling.   Praise
the Lord !   Another conductor taking the train on, I was
prevented working in some of the cars that day.   But at
every stopping-place of note I went out to distribute the
tracts.   Many were in this way made to remember the
mighty work of our dear Jesus for them and for all.
Hallelujah !

I took breakfast in Ogden, one of the strongholds of
Mormonism, preaching Jesus there while waiting.   This
was my first meal in twenty-four hours, and it was rel-
ished.   The next morning Laramie, a city of ten thousand, was reached.   Some friends—Brother Jolly and
wife—were at the train to meet me.   These had been
saved in our holiness meetings in Reno, and were still
"holding the fort."   A time of rejoicing we had upon

meeting. They insisted upon my stopping with them, which I did for some weeks. They were members of "the Church of the first-born, written in heaven," and were sweet singers, singing with "the spirit" and "the understanding." Their practice was to visit all the churches and volunteer as good soldiers of Christ for singing, prayer, testimony, etc. Plain, unpretending people they were, yet, the Spirit leading them, they succeeded in doing a blessed work on the line of

Holiness,

convicting people in all places where they went of the necessity of obeying the command, "Be ye holy, for I, the Lord your God, am holy." Cottage meetings were the order of their plans for my coming, and these dear ones had so worked that through their invitations many flocked to the meetings to hear the Gospel of Jesus Christ from an experimental standpoint. The following is taken from

The Vanguard,

published under date of April 30, 1890:

A month was spent in Wyoming, in the midst of precious revival seasons among the poor,—one place a log cabin. Just before meeting on a stormy evening we saw a small cloud in the spiritual horizon, and with old-time Methodist impulse we stepped up to a lumber pile near the cabin and drew a long board into the room, placing it in the center upon chairs. Soon the seats all around the wall were filled with representatives from the Methodist, Baptist, Presbyterian, Congregational, Episcopalian and Swede Churches, and some who were not members of any organization. The meeting began and progressed in a fervent spirit, and the invitation was given to all who wanted every wrong in their hearts made right to kneel at the penitent form. All but one, a Baptist lady, promptly responded, and O, what a volume of prayer rose as the Spirit melted us into oneness. Deep conviction, consecration and faith followed each other in quick succession as Jesus was accepted as our Saviour from all sin. Tears and praises were commingled as sanctification *by faith* was spoken of and believed for and testified to, as thus we asked for "the old paths." Great power and blessing flowed from heart to heart, and we truly felt that Jesus stood "in the midst." Finally the lady who at first rejected the invitation came rushing out and knelt and prayed aloud for a full salvation. All soon gathered around her to blend their supplications with hers for this crowning grace.

These meetings continued one month in Laramie and suburbs. During the daytime we went from house to house scattering the good seed of the Word. Here we found many forms of suffering,—wives deserted, weeping in hunger and in loneliness, with little helpless, needy children dependent upon them. Others were sick as well as poor. Some were wealthy, but scoffing at the offers of mercy. One of these, a minister's daughter, who ascribed her state of unbelief to her father's hypocrisy, we won over to the faith of Jesus. At first she refused to hear us, but patient love won the day. Hallelujah ! In Nebraska, Iowa, Ohio and New York this blessed work went on, and, in fact, all along the Union Pacific Railway line, and many points north and south of it. In Council Bluffs, at the A. M.-E. Church, we were favored in presenting the Gospel fresh and free when a lady, one of the most wealthy in the city, said to us, ''That is the kind we need here.'' Others, with the Holiness pastor, gladly accepted our exhortation. While holding a meeting with some, prisoners, and talking to a minister's son behind the iron grates, he said with much feeling that he was willing to kneel right there and yield up to God but for his lack of confidence in Christians. However, he did yield to some extent to the earnest appeals of some sweet Christian workers, as we held on by faith to rescue this dear boy. We reminded him of our sorrow in being separated from him by the bars, and told him and others with him of the partition which was then dividing them from God, and of the sorrow of the blessed Lord in consequence, and told them how willing and able He was to remove the sins which separated them from Him, if they would only *ask* and *believe*, truly

repenting toward God, and that in that case they would
be infinitely happy even in prison.   And then we sang :

"Were a dungeon thy dwelling
My home it would be,
For its gloom would be sunshine
If I were with Thee" (Jesus).

Assuring them that such was the intensity of joy divine
in union with Jesus. All were touched, and one yielded,
and the dear W. C. T. U. sisters who went with us were
sweetly blessed. A goodly number of meetings were
held in Laramie jails, and sweet was the power of song
by the dear couple referred to, as those dear boys
relented and hoped for a better life. In one meeting
Satan was so angry that one man became much enraged.
He ran wildly up and down the aisles around the cells,
and screamed his bitter curses, desiring to thrust us
through if he only had a dart. We went on praising,
and even he was vanquished and sought his cell in
quietness. Opportunities offered daily in all places where
we stopped,—churches, street-cars, saloons, homes, temperance unions ; and thus it was that "the communica-
tion of our faith was made effectual." We found many
members of Churches who were cold and formal and
lifeless ; but we also found some in every place who were
zealous workers, all aflame with the theme of holiness,
and "who shunned not to declare the whole truth." At
some

CAMP MEETINGS

power was given us every time we spoke or testified to sanctification. O, how the Lord honors this most lustrous doctrine when spoken from the heart, or lived out in the life, however weak the instrument thus used! At Dodson, Ohio, we addressed about one thousand persons in a tabernacle meeting. From recent dentistry work my mouth was sore and almost destitute of teeth; but the brethren heard of my faith and desired me to speak, taking for my theme,

SANCTIFICATION.

I had a fight of faith, feeling that God did not want me to, under such circumstances, speak to such a large audience. But I was willing and complied, asking the Lord to give me the word and "fill my mouth." It seemed that I could do or say nothing, and so I threw myself helplessly upon God, who hath never failed me in time of need. And while sitting in a carriage with dear Brother and Sister Stoker, of Ohio, who took me to the meeting, all at once the passage in Thessalonians came in force by the Spirit: "This is the will of God, even your sanctification: that ye might abstain from fornication: that every one of you might possess his vessel in honor and in sanctification, not in the lust of concupiscence as do the Gentiles: that no man go beyond and defraud his brother ; for God hath not called you to uncleanness but unto holiness."

In our remarks we stated that all along the line from San Francisco to that place we had found many who were interested in the subject, making inquiry and asking the meaning. Whatever it is we see by this passage that it is the *will of God* that *His children should have it.* Hence we should all desire it for that reason, that " *His will* " might be done. We noticed, also, that the term was synonymous with holiness from the last clause,—" for God hath not called you unto uncleanness, but unto holiness." If we were defining the term we would say, it is *death of self*, and life in Christ. It seems from this Scripture that there is one sin which can only be over-thrown by *sanctification*. " *that* ye might abstain from *fornication*." Here is a sin which the emphatic little word " *that*" in the text shows can only be rooted out by the blessing which makes the old corrupt man go,—the blessing of sanctification. This sin is harldy ever preached against. It is avoided, and yet it is the first, the deepest, the direst and the most prevalent at this day. The Lord wants a clean people, a people who turn not "the grace of God into lasciviousness," but who will have the power to "possess their vessel in honor and in sanctification." God's purpose of grace was shown that His was a full and free salvation, and no half-hearted work ; that in one hand He holds out pardon 'and in the other purity, and will not give one unless we are willing to take both. An appeal was made to all who expected to get to heaven to make the necessary preparation and to cry out:

> "O, that I might at once go up,
> No more this side of Jordan stay,
> But now the land possess,
> This moment end my legal years,
> Sorrow and sin and doubts and fears,—
> A howling wilderness."

The few remarks on social purity and the need and the remedy were followed up by more on the same subject from the evangelist in the lead, Brother Brannenburgh, and his coworkers, Sisters Kalb and Smith, and then testimony and praise and song began to God, giving glory. "All with one accord" seemed the order. Many testified to the inward experience of this blessed grace, and the tide of Christian testimony rose powerfully amidst songs of victory and shouts of praise, and the band on the platform seemed filled with holy joy as their inspired music thrilled the vast audience. Sometimes five or six were on their feet at once, burning with joyous desire to own God's power to save, singing:

> "O, wonderful salvation,
> From sin He sets me free,
> For I know that Jesus saves me,
> And that's enough for me."

And thus it is that the Holy Spirit's power comes to honor His pure doctrine of a pure heart and a holy life.

Hallelujah! The ministry and all saved ones should avail themselves of this glorious privilege and be "entirely sanctified," and then fall in line and swell the grand old theme of "holiness unto the Lord" out of hearts full and overflowing with perfect "love divine." Amen!

CLASS MEETINGS.

In various cities these blessed retreats, where "they that feared the Lord, spake often one to another," were found out, visited and used as a rare privilege of doing good by "spreading holiness over these lands." Once and again, over and over, the work of Jesus in cleansing from all sin was reminded them, some of whom understood it and welcomed the testimonies with hearty praises. Others thanked us for our visits, begging us to sojourn with them. In one village a revival broke out in this way, and the entire class *desired* and *sought* the blessing and believed with great joy. A dear young man in the Piqua class, as also others, told us of the good our words had done them. As for us we were greatly blessed in the midst of these endearing scenes, and the childhood days with dear father and mother at our side in their sheltering retreats came vividly to our mind with sweetest contemplation; and our very first testimony—"I love the Lord because he hath heard my voice and my supplications"—came up to mind once more, and again we thanked God for the training He had vouchsafed unto us in our early years by these dear, dear parents, now gone on before. Our old class in Troy, Ohio, was visited after a lapse of many years, and our dear friends in Jesus greeted our good news of "the fullness of the blessing of the Gospel of Christ" with much warmth of love. In all these ministrations, though in much bodily weakness, we realized the fulfillment of the promise to those who obey the word, —

"Go Ye."

And I think that sanctified people should, as much as possible, do this, for we have always found that we were not without honor, except in our own house and in our own country. But one sweet thought about home and home work comes to mind. It is this : our work at home may and is more opposed and less honored, but it also is God's work, and He will take care of it and see to the results.

At My Mother-in-Law's.

In September I reached the home of my husband's mother, where my two stepsons awaited my arrival. The meeting was a pleasant one, entered into with greatest kindness by mother, sons, daughters and grandchildren. This was highly appreciated after our brief stay in New York City, where, as in other places, we scattered some more "seeds of kindness," with the promising results of hope for fruit in eternity. One case

was that of a boy on his way up the Hudson to attend
school at Kingston. I believe he had never been personally dealt with about his soul. As he and I braved
the wind-storm outside in the boat, he listened atten-
tively and accepted my tracts and promised to lay the
matter to heart. He seemed so willing to hear the word,
and was so gentle and courteous assisting us, that we
longed after him, and thought of the one of whom it
was written, that Jesus "beholding him loved him."
And as we two were spared in that storm on North River
that caused so much loss to others, so I hope we will be
found sheltered together in the Rock of Ages on the
day of judgment. The surpassing scenery on that day's
journey up to the Catskills, and the sweet, sweet work
for Jesus, harmonized well as various parties of travelers
accepted with kind appreciation our loving words and
little printed sermons on Jesus' dying love. After a six
weeks' visit and touring in this lovely region, visiting
meetings and speaking in testimony and in exhortation
on the themes which lay nearest to our heart, reminding
all who heard of the importance of preparing to meet
their God, we bade good-by to dear ones, and my husband's sons Arthur, Ken and I started for Nevada.
Stopping the first evening in Albany, we had another opportunity of scattering the truth as it is in Jesus, and of
receiving more kindness from Him through dear friends.
Praise the Lord! It is hoped that some who heard us in
that city will be saved.

Across the Continent

and home again.   On October 15, 1889, leaving Albany we
took a section in the Phillips' excursion train west bound.
We started in the midst of a cold rainstorm, but *as usual*
we left the storm behind, and the main trip was excellent
as to weather, and withal very pleasant to me.   The dear
boys had made up their minds secretly not to be recon-
ciled to me, but, on the other hand, to test my powers of
grace to the utmost extent.   To this end they would let
me set up the heavy table at meal time and do all the
service.   When night came and they went to their berth
above, instead of walking up the stepladder in an orderly
manner they would step on the lower bed and then reach
up and take hold of the curtain pole and swing off and
land all in a tumble in their berth, and so on.   While
they had no word of conversation for me they were very
affable to all others, making the distinction at times very
painful to behold.   Each of them was seen at the card
tables to my trial.   Neither of them had ever as yet
sought the Lord.   The former was thirteen and the latter
sixteen years of age.   They knew of my manner of life.
The adversary seemed determined to make a gulf between
me and them, and under his influence they seemed to
forget or to distort the motives which led to years of
prayer for them, accompanied by labors, messages and
constant tokens of disinterested love for the little orphans
in the distance.   Strange to say all these things seemed

regarded with hatred instead of love. When these things were revealed to me I would go off into the dressing-room and kneel and pray and praise and supplicate for them, and get a good reward of tenderest blessing. One day a lady in the train came into our car where we were taking dinner. It was on Sunday. She seemed to understand the "salvation look," and, though a stranger to me, she assured me that she knew and had heard me, and desired me to come into her car and hold a meeting, promising voluntary financial aid for the mission work. The dear boys poorly covered the scorn which would show upon their lips at such times. I explained to her that I would come and have a talk with her after dinner, which I did, and found her to be one who loved the truth and those who held it forth. Praise services were held at different times that day in the train, and ended up at nightfall by a loud volley from a little company of salvationists who halted in their march while the train stopped in one of the Western cities. This was a good day to us.

O, how eagerly the people reach out the hand of faith to accept God's blessed gospel when it is offered to them fresh and hot from the Spirit's burning power. How they gather around, so hungry and so earnestly looking for something long lost to satisfy the longings of their souls. These indeed seem like little things, and so they

are, but who can compute them in the aggregate. They
are like the verse :

> " Little drops of water,
>   Little grains of sand,
>   Make the mighty ocean
>   And the pleasant land."

Little streamlets of love run through the green
pastures of the soul almost silently, and their low and
sweet music strikes the ear of faith and sets it to heaven's
sweetest melodies :

> " I love to tell the story,
>   'Twill be my theme in glory,
>   To tell the old, old story
>   Of Jesus and His love."

MORE NOTES ON THE WAY.

The boys were so averse to Christian work by me that
I often did my distributing when they were not present,
thus becoming all things unto them, "that by all means
they might be saved." No weariness to me, but peace,
joy, love, bringing to mind the stanza of the Army
song :

> "Joy, joy, wonderful joy ;
>   Peace, peace, naught can destroy ;
>   Love, love, so boundless and free,--·
>   All this the Lord is to me."

12

Day by day my prayers for all with us and elsewhere ascended to the throne, and my nights were spent in restful and refreshing slumber, under the wings of the protecting spirit.   Praise the Lord !   How I love to pour out my soul in adoration to Him who alone is worthy of all honor, dominion, blessing and glory.   Many were the conversations held with the travelers to the land whence no traveler returns.   The narrow way became brighter and more beloved, though at times the attitude of the dear children to me commingled some real sorrow with all.   As A. B. Simpson says in " Walking in the Spirit :"

> " The path of sorrow, and that path alone,
>   Leads to the land where sorrow is unknown ;
>   No traveler ever reached that blessed abode,
>   Who found not thorns and briars in the road.

But all these are occasions to prove the love and faithfulness of God.   The storm-cloud is but the background for the rainbow, and the falling tear but an occasion for the comforter to wipe it away.

> The comfort is in proportion to the sorrow ;
>   There is an equilibrium of joy and sorrow.

As the sufferings of Christ abound in us, so our consolation also abounds in Christ.   As far as the pendulum swings backward, so far it swings forward.   Every trial is therefore a prophecy of blessing to the heart that walks with Jesus."

These thoughts, like many others of that blessed man, have been realized oftimes by us with sweetest draughts of delight in our inmost depths.   Hallelujah !

Thus the week of travel across the continent afforded varied experiences to us all, and all were made to participate in the mercies of a prosperous journey, free from accident or alarm.   On Monday evening, October 22d, we reached Reno.   I had wired to husband informing him of our near approach.   About this time the boys came to me, and taking seats, looked quite thoughtful.   I suggested for them to go to the toilet-room and brush their clothes and refresh themselves.   Arthur, always the first to speak, remarked, "I washed this morning." This intelligence was hastily followed up by Ken, who said, "I'm not going to clean up till I get home."

I understood them, and answered by silence.   They soon departed, and came back prepared to meet their papa, whom they had not seen since babyhood.

The train stopped.   The porter handed us out, and a happy meeting soon took place, whence we went to the hotel, awaiting our home, which had been in the mean time rented, to be vacated.

Now began a fight of faith on a new line, and a severe conflict it proved to be.   God was with us, and victory came.   Soon the boys were starting for heaven, at least in an outward way.   Slow was the work, but to-day we look back over the three years just past and see work which we believe will stand in eternity and prove the grace of our dear Lord. The profession which was made at first was not as real and deep as at this writing, and we are asking for, working for, and trusting for, better things on before.

A testimony from the *Vanguard*, published in St. Louis, bearing date April 30, 1891, will show something of Arthur's spiritual status, and it is believed he is still trusting in God.

TESTIMONY.

I am fourteen years old. I have given myself to God and His work, I was taken into the M.-E. Church in full connection and baptized, but it did me no good. Then I was taken sick with the typhoid fever, and I promised God if He would restore me to health I would serve Him. Then I got well and went along in my old rut. Every little while my promise came to my mind. It came to me, also, that "He that covereth his sins shall not prosper, but whoso confesseth and forsaketh them shall find mercy" (Prov. xxviii : 13). Then I confessed my sins and forsook them, and I believe Jesus saves me from all my sins. Mother and I go out in mission work together, visiting the sick and the poor, and distributing tracts to the passengers on the trains. We are sweetly blessed. Praise the Lord! Pray for me that I may prove faithful.

Yours, in Jesus' name,

C. ARTHUR PECK.

From Ken, the eldest son, we have just received a letter full of contrition and a hungering after God. Now we are claiming these dear children for Him who *loves them and gave Himself for them.* Dear Jesus, let us not be disappointed in that day "when Thou makest up Thy jewels," but "spare them as a father doth a son who serveth him." Amen!

A CALL FROM MISSIONARIES

came to me in the summer of 1889, to collect funds to defray the expenses of some workers in India, Africa and other points. While I had always given my mite to this and other good causes, it seemed a hard thing to ask for money from others right in the place where one lived and suffered persecution. But they had asked, and I must obey. So down on my knees I went and got a blessed start, and proceeded at once on my errand of love. The first, a neighbor, a Catholic, was called úpon. A bright piece of silver was placed in my hands, and then, at my request, a mother and daughter knelt with me, and Jesus stood in the midst.

Many days were spent in this way. A little purse was collected and sent on, and it is, after a year, a blessed recollection that some dear brethren and sisters in other lands working for Jesus were helped on their journey; and much good came to the donors, some of whom have since themselves engaged in mission work. One name prominent is Miss Eva Quaiffe, who for years stood at the head of the music department in Whitaker Hall, Reno. She is now in a training home for Christians, and testifies that "she is only too glad to work for God." She was one of the happy number who began believing for entire sanctification during Brother Newton's meetings in Nevada.

Too much cannot be said right here about the good influence of those meetings, the fruits of which are ripening into precious spiritual fruit. Others of the donors have since given liberally to other good causes, and are learning rapidly the science of "giving," and some precious souls of that number are to-day looking unto Jesus with a hope of heaven, and have subscribed for Christian journals, and are regular attendants at the Army meetings. Glory to God!

HOLINESS LITERATURE.

Under trying circumstances the Spirit has, from time to time, when work in other channels seemed blocked up, led us to go from house to house taking subscriptions for *salvation*, *holiness* and *faith* journals, and similar literature in book form. This we believe to have done a vast amount of good. Hundreds of avenues have in this way been opened up, the influence of which extended thousands of miles away. Some would sign for friends in the distance.

A dear young girl led a meeting last night in the Salvation Army who in this way read her first religious news in Martin Wells Knapp's "Revivalist," and books. The dear girl referred to has just been converted. She has for years been a neighbor, and the subject of our prayers. Praise the Lord! Many similar instances might be enumerated, and this little line of work has never been so widely extended as at the present writing.

"THE GUIDE TO HOLINESS,"

by Palmer & Hughes, has now found its way to a number of homes in Reno. The *Pacific War Cry* has a large circulation. The *Vanguard*, of the F. M. Church, and countless other good things, come to this place in our daily mails, thus agitating precious souls all about us to the necessity of preparing for

ETERNITY.

The immense amount of evil literature which is constantly sowed abroad over the land demands a mighty counteraction on this line of work for God. It is hoped that, as people will read, the Holy Spirit may supply them with such reading matter as will lead them to

Bancroft

GOD'S WORD,

there to anchor their souls for eternity. This end is being reached. The word is being exalted, and O, that every one who reads it may *ask for the Holy Spirit to teach them* and *make it vital to their hearts*, remembering the words of our Saviour : "If ye, being evil, know how to give good gifts unto your children, how much more shall the Father which is in heaven give the Holy Spirit to them that ask Him?" This is what the people everywhere—all classes—need; the word made "quick and powerful to them, sharper than any two-edged sword." It is by the spirit alone that they can realize that the word of God is "spirit and life;" that it is "the power of God unto salvation to every one that believeth." We can, it is true, speak to the *outer* ear, but only God can speak to the *inner* consciousness, and awaken from the dead the millions of precious blood-bought souls, who cry for the "peace" He alone can give, and the fullness of joy which is realized only in his presence.

Dear Lord, speed on this blessed consummation of union with Thy bride—Thy ransomed church. Amen !

STRENGTH OF MUSCLE

is increased by muscular exercise, so spiritual power is increased by work for God. The sweet "secret" is to be found by abiding in Him, and in this "abiding" we are learning more and more the meaning of His words to us when first he betrothed us unto him, and so by this union strength came daily as we have had need. Like a springing fountain the fullness has flowed out through all our being. "Here am I" has been the one cry of our hearts as we saw openings for work in the seed-

Yours and Christs
M. Hannah Peck.   Francis M. Peck

sowing and in the harvest of souls. As a result of the holiness work the

SALVATION ARMY

have entered the fields of Nevada through the direct work of dear Sister S. McConnaughy and others. A large corps has been formed, and additions are going on. Dear husband and I for years have sympathized with their aggressive and self-denying warfare on sin, and our desires, formed when Mr. and Mrs. Booth first opened up their independent soul-saving work in England, have been realized by the privilege of sharing their labors, in a very humble relation, for some years past, insomuch that after much prayer and consideration we—my husband and I—were, on September 22d, admitted into the *Salvation Army*, under the flag, reconsecrating ourselves to God with a fresh impulse springing up within us for an increase of "seed to the sower" and "bread for our food," beseeching Him to "accept us in the beloved," and overshadow us in the future as He hath in the past. We hope ever to remember that our dear Jesus hath come forth as the

"CAPTAIN OF THE HOSTS OF THE LORD,"

and that our fighting henceforth is to be under the banner of "holiness unto the Lord," which is even now thrilling a lost world as the millenial dawn ushers in and " righteousness covers the earth as the waves cover the sea." It is this "power of an endless life" forcing its way up and out of the death of the carnal nature, nurtured, sustained, matured and preserved by power divine, that is to be the secret of the coming glory. Glory to God! Jesus speaks! The Holy Spirit moves! The Father loves! and all are uniting gloriously. And the true saints of God are by the Spirit's power passing the blessed watchword of "perfect love" all along the line. Sinners are yielding, recruits are enlisting, companies are forming, marching orders are being given, volleys of praise are ascending. Let every true soldier of our Lord Jesus look unto our Great Commander, in whom we trust, and

"Put on the whole armour of God, that ye may be able to stand against the wiles of the Devil.

"For we wrestle not against flesh and blood, but against principalities, against powers, against the rulers of the darkness of this world, against spiritual wickedness in high places.

"Wherefore take unto you the whole armour of God, that ye may be able to withstand in the evil day, and having done all to stand.

"Stand, therefore, having your loins girt about with truth, and having on the breastplate of righteousness;

"And your feet shod with the preparation of the Gospel of peace.

"Above all, taking the shield of faith, wherewith ye shall be able to quench all the fiery darts of the wicked.

"And take the helmet of salvation, and the sword of the spirit, which is the word of God.

(Eph. vi: 11–17.)

"And the very God of peace sanctify you wholly : and I pray God your whole spirit, soul and body be preserved blameless unto the coming of our Lord Jesus Christ.

"Faithful is He that calleth you who also will do it."

(Thess. v : 23, 24.)

ROBED AND RESTING.

Tune: "He Will Hide Me."

BY F. M. PECK.

Once I was away from Jesus,
    Drifting on the billows' foam,
And my bark was almost dashing·
    On the rifted rocks alone.

CHORUS.

Jesus saves me, yes, He saves me,
    Gives me grace for every hour ;
Jesus keeps me, yes, he keeps me,
    By His ever living power.

Jesus found me poor and needy,
    Took me in His tender care,
Brought me to His royal palace,
    Made me welcome to a share.

Jesus put new robes upon me,
    Robes of pure and spotless white ;
And my soul that sat in darkness
    He hath changed to sit in light.

Now I am no longer drifting ;
    I am rescued from the wave,
Still upon life's ocean sailing,
    Giving only Jesus praise.

Safe in Jesus now I'm resting ;
  In the rifted Rock I'll hide,
Till I've passed beyond the Jordan
  Of death's cold and chilling tide.

JESUS CALLS.   ·

" Come unto me all, ye that labor and are heavy laden, and I will
give you rest.
  "Take my yoke upon you, and learn of me ; for I am meek and
lowly in heart : and ye shall find rest unto your souls.
  "For my yoke is easy, and my burden is light."

(Matt. xi : 28–30.)

O, sinner, come to Jesus,
  Make haste and come "to-day ;"
Your time is swiftly gliding,
  There's danger in delay.

Why will you slight His mercy ?
  His spirit moves you now.
O, grieve Him not, I pray you,
  Repent, believe just *now.*

His yoke you'll find most easy,
  His burden very light ;
Come wash your garments in His blood,
  And walk with Him in white.

Then gird His sword upon you,
  And forth to battle go,
To slay the wrong, defend the right,
  And conquer every foe.

He's calling now for soldiers,
  For loyal heart and true ;
His service is most blessed,
  And fraught with honor too.

I love to live for Jesus,
  Because He died for me ;
He fills my soul with peace and joy,
  From sin He sets me free.

THE TWO BLESSINGS.

Wherefore let him that thinketh he standeth take heed, lest he fall (1 Cor. x : 12).

In the blessing of pardon, or "justification by faith," or "the washing of regeneration," or "the heart sprinkled from an evil conscience," or "forgiveness of sins," which are all synonymous terms, the happy one for a time seems satisfied, and really "thinks" that he *stands*. And no wonder, for he feels so clean, so sweet, so pure, so bright and so peaceful. But, after all, he is but a little child. He has just been "born of the spirit." I say again, he is only a child. He "speaks" as such and "understands" as such. This is a gate to be gone through. "Except ye be converted and become as little children ye shall not enter into the kingdom of heaven" (Matt. xviii : 3). Paul makes a distinction, as do all who receive both blessings. Hence, in Romans v he speaks of "this grace wherein we *stand*." Not *think* we stand, but *stand*. In the first case, there is still lodged within the soul, a great evil, the "carnal mind," which is "enmity against God, for it is not subject to the law of God, neither indeed can be" (Rom. viii : 7). This, also, must be destroyed "*by faith,*" at which period in the Christian walk the saved one has the "witness of God, the spirit," who also hath wrought the work from the beginning—carrying it forward—that his "love is made perfect," his "heart purified by faith," his soul "renewed in the image of God." Now, when this great work of God takes place, the sanctified one *knows* that he "stands,' and he rejoices in hope of the glory of God ; and not only so, but he glories in tribulation also, knowing that tribulation worketh patience, and patience experience, and experience hope ; and hope maketh not ashamed, because the love of God is shed abroad in his heart by the Holy Ghost given unto him. " Therefore, being justified by faith, we have peace with God through our Lord Jesus Christ, by whom also we have access *by faith into this grace, wherein we stand*" (Rom. v : 1, 2).